HIS BROTHER'S WIFE

A BILLIONAIRE ROMANCE

MICHELLE LOVE

HOT AND STEAMY ROMANCE

CONTENTS

Made in "The United States" by:

Michelle Love

© Copyright 2021

ISBN: 978-1-64808-779-0

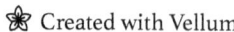 Created with Vellum

BLURB

I'm going to take Amalia for her very first time.

Hell, I might even fall in love with her for MY very first time.
I know it from the moment I first lay eyes on her seductive curves.
There's only one problem.
That moment happens to be when she is walking down the aisle to marry my hateful half brother Jackson.
I'm his illegitimate half-brother, the black sheep playboy of the family.
I'm used to doing what I want.
And now what I want to do is Amalia.
To have my way with her while she submits to my every command.
But her father has sold her off to Jackson as part of a business deal.
Fulfilling our desires could mean she's disowned and Jackson's wrath could destroy both of us.
He'd better be ready for the fight of his life because I'm going to take what I want, which is Amalia over my knee and then on her own knees for me.
And I know from the look in her sultry eyes that she wants to give me what I want, no matter the cost.

When beautiful classical pianist, Amalia Rai, marries billionaire Jackson Gallo, it is not a happy union. Amalia's father has blackmailed his daughter into marrying the man who can save his company—and in return, he will allow Ama's younger sister, Selima, to divorce her abusive husband.

As she walks down the aisle, Ama's life is changed forever when she sees Enda—Jackson's illegitimate, Italian half-brother. The attraction between them is obvious.

Beginning a sensual, erotic affair with Enda, desperate to relieve the tension from her sham of a marriage, Ama falls in love with him, but when Jackson finds out about the affair, his rage is all-consuming.

Fleeing to Italy with Enda, Ama begins a new life, making friends with Enda's best friends, Raffaelo Winter and his lovely wife, Inca. Happier than ever, she is shattered when, after months of silence, Jackson takes his revenge, shattering everyone and everything Ama cares about ...

Can Ama find the strength to fight for the people she loves and live happily ever after with the man of her dreams?

1

PART ONE

Not for the first time, Amalia Rai gazed in the mirror and wondered how the hell she had gotten here. *This is the twenty-first century, right?* And, yet, she, a successful classical pianist and music professor, was about to be married to a man she barely knew—and who she could barely stand.

Amalia closed her eyes. She could hardly stand to look at the sadness in her own eyes. At twenty-seven, she had accomplished so much and had thought herself free of her controlling father and all the bullshit that went on in their family. If it hadn't been for her desperation to save her little sister's life, she would never have agreed to this.

But her father held all the cards. He would not allow Selima to divorce her abusive husband unless Amalia agreed to marry Jackson Gallo—her father's rival in business and the man who had nearly brought her father to his knees. When Gallo offered Gajendra Rai a lifeline—give him his eldest daughter in marriage, and he'll give Gajendra a multimillion dollar cash –injection—Gajendra had not hesitated in going to Amalia and demanding she marry Jackson.

Amalia had turned him down flat. That she and her father were not close was an understatement. For months, she had held out, until the day Selima had called her from the emergency room of the hospital. Her husband had beaten her so badly that she could barely speak, but just sob over the phone to her sister. Amalia went to her and was horrified by her injuries and by what she had been through. Gajendra, though, refused to let Selima divorce her husband ...unless Amalia married Jackson.

Desperate, Amalia agreed, and now, in a few minutes, she would take her father's arm and walk down the aisle in the church Jackson's family had built in their luxurious compound on the outskirts of San Francisco. *A prison, not a compound*, thought Amalia as she straightened the wedding dress that had cost seven times her salary. Her father had paid, of course, and although Amalia would have preferred to marry in the traditional Indian attire befitting her heritage, her father insisted that a white dress would be more suitable for the society pages.

Amalia shrugged to herself now. What did it matter? This wasn't a real wedding and it wouldn't be a real marriage. She had made it clear to Jackson that under no circumstances would the marriage be consummated. Jackson had laughed, and she knew he thought she was joking. He would find out tonight that she was deadly serious.

Jackson Gallo was handsome in a bland, preppy way. The youngest son of billionaire property magnate Macaulay Gallo, Jackson was often to be found in the pages of gossip magazines, romancing some of the world's most beautiful women. When he had laid eyes on Amalia at a benefit gala where she was performing, he'd pursued her relentlessly until Amalia had grown frightened of his vehemence. She had finally thought he'd gotten the message she wasn't interested when the call from her father came. Jackson had been victorious when Ama had agreed to marry him, but for the life of her, she couldn't understand why he would settle on her. Yes, she was a renowned pianist and a very successful professor of music at The San Francisco Conservatory of Music. Yes, she knew she was considered a beautiful woman, with her creamy coffee-and-pink skin, bright green eyes, long, wavy, dark hair, and curvaceous body, but to society and Jackson's world, she was completely indifferent.

A knock came at the door and her sister, dressed in a simple lilac silk sheath, came in and smiled at her. "Hey, sis ... are you nearly ready? Dad's hovering outside."

Ama smiled at her. "Almost." She sighed and stood. Selima came up to her and studied her.

"It's not too late, you know. We can skip out of here and escape somewhere hot."

Ama laughed sadly. "And live on what, Lima?"

Selima shrugged, but her eyes were sad. "I hate that you're doing this for me."

Ama hugged her sister. "I swear, knowing that you'll be free of that bastard is the only good thing about this."

Selima nodded. "Thank you, Ama. I mean it. And look, the prenup says ..."

"I'm trapped for two years." Ama tried to make a joke of it. "Trapped, but living in luxury. How many women would kill to be me right now?"

Selima's nose wrinkled. "With that creep?" Selima had as much of a low opinion of Jackson as Amalia did. Her smile brightened. "*Olivier*, on the other hand ..."

Olivier Gallo was Jackson's older brother, and Ama had grown very fond of him. He was in his early forties and a workaholic, but kind and quiet. He was the only one in the family who didn't stand for Jackson's arrogance or posturing, and there were many times when he'd met Amalia's gaze over the family dinner table and rolled his eyes at what Jackson was bloviating about on that particular night.

And yes, Olivier was gorgeous and tall, with dark hair and brown eyes, but there was sadness in him that Amalia didn't understand. Macaulay had once told Amalia that Olivier had been particularly close to his mother, who had died giving birth to Jackson, who was thirteen years younger than Olivier. Amalia was curious about that, and about the fact that Olivier seemed to have no time for anything else, but work in his life.

Selima had a huge crush on the older Gallo brother. She grinned at Amalia now. "I bagged the seat next to him, too. Hey, isn't today when we all meet the black sheep?"

Amalia nodded. Enda Gallo was the middle brother ...well, middle *half*-brother, the result of an extramarital affair Macaulay had had with an Italian actress. Amalia had never met him, but knew he kept to himself, mostly living in Italy. Since Enda had been ignored by his father for the first thirty years of his life, it was only because Olivier had reached out to him seven years ago that Enda had finally been brought into the family fold and had reconciled with his father. Jackson couldn't stand him, always referring to him as 'the bastard' and badmouthing him. Amalia, having never met Enda Gallo, was already disposed to liking him because Jackson hated him so much.

The clock struck noon and Amalia sighed. "Let's get this thing over with."

GAJENDRA LAID his daughter's arm over his and smiled at her. "You make me very proud today, Amalia."

Amalia didn't reply, keeping her expression blank as they walked down the long aisle of the church. At the altar, she could see Jackson waiting, a supercilious smile on his face. Olivier, his best man, smiled at her and winked. Amalia gave a little sigh. If she could just hang out and be friends with Olivier, then maybe she would get through this. There were hundreds of people there, most of whom she didn't know. Some of her friends from the conservatory sat on the left-hand side of the church. Christina, her best friend, a no-nonsense Korean cellist, made a face at her and Amalia tried not to laugh. Christina was the only one of her friends who knew the real reason behind this marriage. Amalia had told her she wasn't going to ask her to be maid of honor, "because I want to save you for my *real* wedding someday."

Christina had grinned and toasted her. "Hell, yes. Let's drink to that."

God, thought Amalia. Their nights out drinking seemed so far away now. Would Jackson stop her from enjoying her freedom? Probably.

Amalia was nearly at the altar now, and she saw Macaulay Gallo smiling at her. Despite his weaknesses, she liked the old man ...he just had no idea how to raise children and had left all the responsibility of the Gallo estate to Olivier. Amalia smiled back at him now. She could have worse as a father-in-law.

Then her eyes met the man standing next to Macaulay and her breath caught in her throat. Tall, athletic, with dark curls messy around his head, he glowered at her, his bright green eyes intensely fierce. His face was set grimly and he looked like the most dangerous man she'd ever seen.

And the most devastatingly handsome ...

Amalia stumbled a little and her father steadied her. The man, who she guessed *had* to be Enda Gallo, stared at her. *He hates me ...he hates me* ...she thought, her heart sinking. There was no mistaking the man's expression. Loathing. He looked like he wanted to kill her ...

Don't be stupid. He doesn't know you. And you don't know him. Maybe that's just how his face is; moody and dark, with a definite edge. His sensual mouth was set in a straight line, as if he were gritting his teeth, and Amalia felt as if she could feel the heat of anger coming from him. As she passed by him, she breathed in a wave of woodsy, clean cologne. It sent her senses reeling, and her body reacted, her nipples hardening and a pulse beating between her legs. He radiated pure animal, dangerous sex.

Even as she was saying her vows in a monotone, she could feel his eyes on her. As Jackson, his face set in the fakest smile she had ever seen, recited his own vows, Amalia chanced a glance at Enda Gallo. His eyes were fixed on her face, and briefly, Amalia entertained the fantasy that he would stop the wedding, grab her hand, and run away with her, intending to take her away and fuck her senseless ...

Woah ...where did that come from? Ama struggled to pull her attention back to the present and realized, with a sinking heart, that she'd missed the moment. Her last moment of single life.

She was married.

.   .   .

THE GREETING LINE, the dinner, and the speeches were all a blur. Ama didn't bother to listen to the platitudes of her new husband. Even Macaulay seemed a little subdued. It was only when Olivier stood to speak that she took notice. He said all the things that were expected of him, and Ama could see he struggled with finding good things to say about his brother. When he turned to her, though, his eyes softened.

"And to my new sister ...I am very glad to have you in our lives, Amalia. We are privileged to have someone so brilliant, kind, and independent. I can assure you, sweetheart, that we will always care for you ...and encourage you in your career and aspirations."

His meaning was clear—*don't worry, we won't let Jackson control you*—and Ama smiled back at him warmly, mouthing 'thank you' to him. She had an ally. It made her feel more secure. She saw Enda Gallo at the back of the ballroom, propped against the bar. He met her gaze and Ama felt a flush creep up her face. Why did he have such a visceral, feral effect on her? It was a new feeling for her. She looked away, and when she looked back, he had gone.

THE RECEPTION SEEMED to go on for days, and by midnight, Amalia was drooping. She had changed from her wedding dress into a simple, dark burgundy slip dress, freeing her hair from the intricate bun she had worn for the ceremony and pulling it over one shoulder.

She was tired of Jackson parading her around as if she were an object, and when she returned to the ballroom, she sought out her sister and Christina who were huddled in the corner, clearly making fun of the prissy society people.

"Ama!" Christina was already drunk, and Amalia grinned at her. Christina hugged her friend and looked her up and down. "That's better. You look more like you now."

"Agreed," Ama laughed, but in the next moment, she felt Jackson's hand on her upper arm pulling her away from her friends.

"What the fuck are you wearing?"

Ama wrenched her arm out of his grip. "It's called a dress, Jackson."

"On your feet," he said darkly and pointed down to her comfortable and admittedly well-worn flat pumps. "Go and change into heels, right now."

Ama looked him in the eye. "I will not. I've had heels on all day and now I want to be comfortable. It's after midnight, Jackson. I've played the part you wanted long enough for one day."

Jackson's eyes were fierce on hers. "May I remind you, you are my wife now?"

Ama's smile was cold. "Wife. Not *staff*, Jackson. Did you hear me say 'obey' in my vows? No, you did not. Now, some of your guests are looking at us, probably wondering why I look so pissed off. Want me to tell them why?"

Jackson's jaw clenched. "We'll talk about this later. In bed."

He stalked off and Ama saw him switch on the charm instantly as he spoke to the guests who had been watching them. Ama felt sick. *No.* No way would they do *anything* in bed. Ever.

She returned to her friends, but soon excused herself. She needed to be alone for a few moments to get some air. She slipped out into the beautiful gardens surrounding the mansion and walked quickly down to the little Japanese garden that had been her go-to place for escaping Jackson since they'd become engaged.

There were a few lanterns giving the place a soft glow and she sat down on one of the stone seats and closed her eyes, taking a deep breath in. Silence. Bliss. She only heard the tiny trickle of the water feature.

Then she caught a breath of cigarette smoke and opened her eyes. Enda Gallo stood on the other side of the garden, staring at her. Ama's heart began to pound against her ribs and she stood. She didn't know what to do. Running would seem rude, but the expression on Enda's face was ...what?

She turned to leave, and in a flash, he was beside her. Trapping her against a tree in the cage of his arms, he gazed down at her. Ama couldn't look away. God, he was *beautiful* ...those eyes, that craggy, yet boyish face. She noticed he had a half moon scar at the corner of his right eye, and without thinking, she traced the line of it with her finger. His eyes never left hers. Ama could barely breathe, such was the tension between them.

Enda bent his head and brushed his lips against hers. Ama froze. What the hell was going on? Was he testing her?

He kissed her again, and this time, she couldn't help but kiss him back. His lips were soft, but his kiss was rough---almost violent---and she found her fingers twisted in his dark curls as they embraced. When she felt, his hands push up her dress, a jolt of panic slid through her, but then he pressed his body against hers and she was lost. She had never wanted anyone as badly as she wanted Enda Gallo right here, right now. His fingers were caressing her through her panties and she felt herself dampen with longing. Cupping his cock through his pants, she marveled at the size of him and panicked at the same time. Could she do this? Should she?

Could she really, *finally*, lose her virginity to her brother-in-law on her *wedding* night?

Enda's eyes were questioning now ...and somehow Ama knew that if she asked him to stop, he would, without question.

But she didn't want him to stop. She wanted him here, *now* ...

Enda swept her off her feet and onto one of the stone tables that framed the little garden. He unzipped his fly, freed his diamond-hard cock from his pants, and climbed on top of her.

Ama felt like this was a dream—a fantasy—right up until Enda Gallo thrust into her and she gave a little cry of pain. It faded quickly, and then all she felt was an all-consuming pleasure as he made love to her, kissing her tenderly, his cock driving deeper and deeper into her with every stroke. His hands pinned hers to the table, his eyes locked onto hers as they moved together, her legs wrapped around his hips. Ama felt her orgasm build, and when she came, her back arched up off the table, pressing against him as she gasped and shuddered. Enda kissed her passionately, then raised his head and groaned as he too came, pumping thick, creamy semen deep into her belly. He gave her no time to recover; his mouth found her clit and teased it until she was weeping with desire, and then his cock was inside her again driving her onwards and onwards, toward her climax.

Afterward, he pulled her into his arms and kissed her. He still had not spoken one word to her. He touched her face once more ...and then he was gone.

Ama, her legs still shaking, sat down quickly on the bench, blinking. Did that really just happen? Her body answered—*god, yes, yes* ...

She had just fucked Enda Gallo ...or *he* had fucked *her*. Ama gave a disbelieving laugh. She sat there for a further five minutes, then made her way slowly back inside the house. Most of the guests had gone now and Christina was looking for her.

"Have to go, sweets, before I drink this place dry." She hugged Amalia, then studied her. "Hey, are you okay? You look weird."

Ama blinked, then tried to smile. "Just tired, babe. Look, promise me we'll get together for lunch on Monday."

"Promise."

She went back into the main ballroom, her heart thumping at the thought of seeing Enda in there. But he was nowhere to be seen. Jackson came over to her. "Our guests have left—would have been nice of you to say goodbye. I hope you'll be more sociable in the future."

"Fine." She didn't want to argue. "Goodnight, Jackson."

He caught her arm. "Where are you going?"

"To bed."

"To *our* bed."

Ama sighed. He would never stop trying, would he? "No, Jackson. To *my* room. I told you once, and I meant it. I will never, *ever* have sex with you. Find one of your many admirers—I assume you've worked your way through most of them anyway. I'm sure one of them will be up for it."

Jackson stared at her, his face angry, then stepped closer to her. "You will submit to me one day, little girl, or I'll break you. I swear I will."

Ama wasn't impressed. "Go away, *little boy*. You don't scare me."

She turned and walked out of the room, running lightly up the huge staircase, hoping he wouldn't follow her. Selima was in her room, packing her wedding dress away. "Dad's just bringing the car around." Selima had tears in her eyes as she hugged her sister. "I'll never be able to repay you for what you've done for me, Ama. Never. I just pray you find some happiness."

Ama held her sister, feeling the tears threatening again. "Go along now. Dad's probably waiting. I'll see you soon."

Selima nodded. "I love you."

"Love you too."

ALONE, she locked the door and put a chair up against it. She didn't trust Jackson not to have a spare key. There was no way she was letting him in. Sure, enough, a half hour later, as she walked out of the shower, toweling her long hair dry, the door handle rattled. She smirked to herself as she heard him curse, but he soon gave up.

Amalie sat down on the bed. She was married ...and had lost her virginity all in one day. And to two different men. *What the hell was I thinking?*

She already knew she regretted one of those things ...and it wasn't anything to do with Enda Gallo.

OLIVIER GALLO DROVE into town and was at the restaurant fifteen minutes before his half-brother arrived. He stood to hug Enda, who clapped him on the back. "Hey, brother, good to see you."

"You too." They sat, and Olivier beckoned the waiter over. "Could we have the drinks menu please?"

"No need," Enda said in his deep, accented tones, "Red. Third down from the top."

Both brothers laughed, and the waiter nodded. He knew these Gallo brothers—they had been coming to this restaurant for a few years now and were good tippers. They treated him with respect, unlike their asshole brother Jackson.

The restaurant itself was mid-range and less flashy than the places Jackson liked. It had a frontage, which opened out onto a jetty overlooking of the Bay. They sat outside so Enda could smoke. Olivier grinned at him as he lit up a cigarette. "You ever going to give up?"

Enda squinted through the smoke. "Probably not."

Olivier grinned. "Fair enough. How have you been? I didn't get to see you much at the wedding."

"As I recall, you were doing your best man thing, trying to keep the toddler under control."

Olivier rolled his eyes. "Mostly for Amalia's benefit. Poor kid looked shell-shocked."

"She's no kid."

Olivier's eyes opened wide. "You don't like her?"

"I didn't say that. I just meant, she's a grown woman. She knew what she was getting into."

Olivier chewed his lip for a moment. "She did it for her sister, Enda."

Enda nodded. "I'm just saying ...it sucks for her."

"Yep."

They paused while the waiter brought their wine and they ordered their food. Enda sat back and took a slug of red wine. "She's beautiful."

"Who?"

Enda rolled his eyes. "Our brother's new wife."

"Of course. Sorry. Yes, she is. Also, brilliant, funny, and smart."

Enda nodded. "She also seems to have ...what is the word ... empathy?" He pronounced it 'em-patty.'

"Like I said, she's a sweetheart."

"You like her?" Enda grinned at Olivier's eye-roll.

"As my *sister*, yes." Olivier chuckled. "If it's any of your business, I'm seeing someone."

"Oh, yes? Wait, please tell me it's not that blonde from the reality show?"

Olivier laughed. "No. That was ...jeez, what was I thinking?

Anyway, no. She's a journalist from San Diego. Helena. Early days, but yeah, she's cool."

Enda looked skeptical. "A journalist?"

Olivier grinned. "Not that kind. She's focused on business and financial stuff. I like her." Their food arrived then—steamed salmon for Olivier, rare, bloody steak and garlic butter for Enda. Olivier shook his head, laughing. "Dude, you are a walking heart attack."

Enda grinned, his smile lighting up his intense features. "Hedonism is my default position."

They ate in silence for a few minutes, then Olivier cleared his throat. "So, what did you think?"

"Of what?"

"Amalia."

"She's beautiful."

"You said that."

Enda shrugged. "I don't know her, Olly. I barely spoke to her. If you tell me she is a good person, I believe you."

Olivier speared some asparagus with his fork. "Enda ...I'm worried. Lately, Jackson has been more ...out of control than normal. This deal he made with Amalia's father ...you know he engineered it so that Ama was practically forced into this marriage."

"*Ama*, is it now?" Enda teased his older half-brother, but then his smile faded. "That sounds just like Jackson, though. He always got what he wanted. Didn't matter how."

Olivier sighed. "I know, but this is a person we're talking about. If and when she does something he doesn't like ...Enda, he has addictions. Cocaine, for one. And this thing with Ama ...he's *obsessed* with her. I'm worried."

Enda looked away from his brother's gaze. "What can I do?"

"Stick around 'Frisco for a few months. Help me keep Jackson on a steady keel. See how the land lies."

Enda closed his eyes and pinched the bridge of his nose. Olivier could see his internal struggle. Enda hated Jackson with the fury of a thousand suns, but he didn't owe Amalia Rai anything. He didn't even know her.

"I'm thinking about dad in this too. If Jackson were to do something rash or worse, Dad wouldn't survive it. I'm not saying you owe him anything either, but for me, maybe." Olivier's voice was low and Enda nodded.

"I will stay. I can oversee the business from here. We have been thinking of opening an office here ...maybe it's time. I'll talk to Raffaelo in the morning."

JACKSON GALLO WAS FRUSTRATED. It had been a month since the wedding and Ama had barely spoken to him, let alone touched him. She attended functions with him and behaved impeccably, but he couldn't bust through those walls of hers. Her bedroom door remained locked and barred ...if it wasn't for the fact that his father slept in the same house, and that their staff also were there at night, he would have busted down that door and taken her.

But he knew she would leave him if he forced himself on her. So, to satisfy his aching balls, he had started fucking other women almost immediately after the wedding. If Ama guessed, she didn't seem to care, and it drove him mad.

It had been particularly galling that, since the wedding, Gajendra Rai's business had flourished, being linked to the Gallo name. And Amalia's sister, Selima, had settled into her new life as a student in Los Angeles. It seemed to Jackson that Amalia had reaped the rewards of their union, while he still hadn't.

He sat in his office now and decided to call her. She picked up the phone eventually, sounding harassed. "What do you want, Jackson?"

He rankled. "Well, for one, I'd like you to speak to me with respect."

Amalia sighed. "I'm busy, Jackson, What do you want?" There was no noticeable shift in her tone.

"I would like to take you out to dinner tonight."

"Fine."

"Be ready at eight."

"Fine." The phone clicked in his ear. So much for sweet nothings.

Jackson put his phone down and smiled to himself. He'd actually arranged to have dinner with his brothers that night, but he couldn't resist bringing Ama and showing her off to them. *Look at my glorious wife. Look how beautiful she is.*

Suddenly an idea struck him and he laughed to himself. Flicking through his contacts on his phone, he made the call, smiling to himself.

AMA SAW Enda as soon as they entered the restaurant and knew Jackson had set this up on purpose. "I didn't know we were having dinner with your brothers."

Jackson smiled. "Family time."

Ugh. More like bragging time. She was being trotted out like a prize horse. But at the moment, she could think of nothing else, but Enda Gallo's eyes on her. God, she'd forgotten just how gloriously good looking he was. Olivier stood and kissed her cheek, and then she was in front of Enda. He leaned in and kissed her cheek. "*Bella.*"

That voice—deep, mellifluous, accented—was dripping with sex. She wondered if he could see the blatant longing in her eyes.

She was mostly silent through dinner, ignoring Jackson as much as she could, to Enda and Olivier's obvious amusement. Olivier distracted them all with jokes, and Enda, too, she found, was fun to be around. He and Olivier were obviously close, and both busted Jackson's chops, which was fine by her. For once, she saw Jackson as he really was—the baby of the family. Despite his bragging, he was still just a little kid. Olivier and Enda were men. She couldn't help, but compare them. Jackson, his dark blonde hair slicked back; Oliver, neatly trimmed beard and dark brown eyes, so beautifully dressed. Then there was Enda—his looks had a wildness to them, a devil-may-care look. He oozed easy sex appeal. *God, I want you,* Ama thought, then pushed the thought away. He was off-limits. At least, *now* he was.

"What are you smiling at?" Jackson demanded of her suddenly, and Ama jumped slightly. Jackson's arm had been along the back of her chair, possessively, and her back ached from sitting forward to avoid him touching her.

"Just marveling at how different you are from your brothers," she said coolly. *You don't snap at me like that. Ever,* her eyes said, and Jackson backed off. "If you'll excuse me, I must go freshen up."

In the bathroom, she splashed some water on her face and tried to stop thinking about Enda. When she finally got up her courage to go back to the table, she exited the bathroom. She gave a little cry of surprise as two hands gripped her waist from behind and pulled her back into the dark alcove. She turned and saw Enda smiling down at her. "Hello again."

His voice sent thrills through her body, and when he kissed her, she couldn't help, but give a little moan of desire. They were hidden from sight, and when Enda slid his hands under her skirt, Amalia's body reacted, curving into his. "I want you so badly," she whispered, and Enda grinned, his lips rough against hers.

"If it wouldn't get us arrested, *cara mia*, I would fuck you right here. Sadly, I think my brother's suspicions would be aroused."

"I'm not sleeping with him. I don't know why it's important to me that you know that, but it is."

Enda stroked her cheek. "I know, *Bella*. Listen ...I must see you again. Can I come to your office?"

She nodded and gave him the address. "I know this is wrong, but ..."

His lips silenced hers and she could feel his erection through his pants. God, she wanted him so badly. Her skin felt like it was on fire.

She went back to the table a few moments before Enda, but couldn't help but feel that their lust for each other was obvious. Jackson seemed not to notice, though, and when Enda returned, there was nothing in Jackson or Olivier's glances that gave anything away.

Ama felt sick with excitement. He wanted *her* ...what the hell was she supposed to do? She barely knew him, but she knew, without a doubt, that she was falling for Enda Gallo.

. . .

As Olivier and Amalia walked ahead of them, Jackson held Enda back with a touch of a hand. He smiled without humor at his half-brother. "I hope we will see you at the house more often."

Enda looked askance. "That's new. Since when?"

Jackson's expression was mocking. "Now I'm happily married; I just want us to be family. And when my children are born ...well ..." He smiled smugly, and Enda wanted to pound his face in.

"Fine." He turned and walked away, catching up with Olivier and Ama. He had no time for Jackson's games. Since that farce of a wedding, all he could think about was Ama. When he had seen her walking down that aisle, apparently terrified, his heart had started to beat quicker, and when their eyes had met, a thrill of desire had run through him. Later, in the garden, he hadn't been able to help himself when he saw her so sad and so lovely in that slip of a dress, her long hair tumbling around her shoulders. No one that beautiful should be that unhappy. He hadn't meant to kiss her, but when she'd looked up at him, her lovely eyes so troubled, her dusky skin glowing in the low light, her lips so red and plump, it was the most natural thing in the world to kiss her.

As soon as their lips had touched, he had known he was lost. Making love with her ...yes, he should feel guilty, and he would do if it had been any other man's wife. Not that the guilt had stopped him before. But something about Ama was different. He knew it had been an arranged marriage and that she was an unwilling participant in it. And, god, he had wanted her so *badly* ...

He and Olivier said goodbye to Ama and Jackson as they got into their car. Ama met his gaze and smiled slightly. Her eyes told him everything he wanted to know. As they drove away, Olivier sighed. "I hope he treats her right."

"God help him if he doesn't," Enda said darkly.

Olivier studied him. "You don't think ...I mean, the thing with Penelope was years ago. He learned his lesson, right?"

Enda looked at his brother. "God, Olivier, I really hope so."

. . .

THE PACKAGE WAS WAITING for Ama on her desk when she arrived at work the following Monday. Her assistant, Lena, greeted her with a smile "Jeez, Ama, was that the honeymoon? That was quick."

Ama tried to smile. "We've postponed it for a while, because of work. It's no problem, really." Lena didn't need to know Ama had refused to go on honeymoon with Jackson. She had no doubt that if she had been alone with him ...god, she couldn't bear to consider what might happen.

She went into her office and dumped her purse on the desk, glancing at the parcel. The label was handwritten—just her name in a beautiful cursive scrawl. "When did this come?"

Lena grinned. "This morning. Girl, you should have seen the delivery guy. *Gorgeous*. Italian, I think."

She went back out to her desk, not realizing the frenzied excitement that had started in her boss. Ama touched the label, running her finger over her name. Picking it up, she opened the parcel. A burner phone. She switched it on. Only one number was programmed into it, under the name 'He.' Ama smiled. She was really going to do this, wasn't she? Have an affair ...

She thought about Jackson trying once again to get into her bedroom last night and her teeth clenched. *Yes.* She was going to do this. *Hell, yes.*

She closed her office door quietly and pressed the dial button. Her heart was beating against her ribs and adrenaline spiked in her when she heard his voice. "*Cara mia ...*"

"Hey there ...*He*." She chuckled, hearing him laugh.

"I thought that was the safest name I could come up with. How are you today?"

"Better now that I've heard your voice," she said softly, "When can I see you?"

"Can you be free for lunch?"

"I can." God, she felt like a love-struck teenager.

Enda laughed. "Good. Write this address down." He gave her an address in Russian Hill. "Take a cab. I'll meet you there."

. . .

AT NOON, a very nervous, but excited Ama was in a cab, being driven to Russian Hill. When she got there, Enda was waiting outside an apartment building. He took her hand and led her inside. "I rented an apartment. I thought it would be safer."

Ama felt like she was in a dream. In the elevator, Enda took her in his arms and kissed her. 'Hello again," he said softly, and she smiled up at him.

The 'apartment' was, in fact, the penthouse of the building, and Ama stood open-mouthed at the door, suddenly feeling intimidated. Enda laughed. "You live in a mansion and an apartment is what scares you?"

Ama relaxed, chuckling. "Sorry. It's beautiful."

Enda came to her. "*You're* beautiful. This is just bricks and mortar. Come with me."

He led her into the bedroom, beautifully decorated in gray and navy. Enda's fingers were at the belt of her wrap dress. "I'm sorry, *Bella*, I can't wait any longer ..."

Ama gave a soft moan as he pulled open her dress and dropped to his knees, his mouth on her belly, his tongue tracing a circle around her navel. She tangled her fingers in his hair as he pulled down the lacy cup of her bra and took her nipple into his mouth, teasing the small bud until it grew hard and sensitive. She closed her eyes as he did the same to the other nipple, and then he was sliding her panties down and burying his face in her sex.

Holy hell ...the feeling of his tongue sliding along her sex, lashing around her clitoris, then plunging deep into her red and swollen cunt was intoxicating. Her limbs felt they were liquefying.

Enda pushed her gently onto the bed and spread her legs wide, eager to taste her further. He began to slide two fingers in and out of her. Ama was gasping, her entire body aflame, and she came shuddering and moaning.

"I want to taste you," she whispered, and Enda grinned. He stripped down quickly as Ama shed the rest of her clothes, sitting up, then taking him in her mouth. She had no idea if she was doing it right, but she went with her instincts, tracing the shaft up and down with her tongue and teasing the tip. She heard Enda moan apprecia-tively as she began to move his cock in and out of her mouth, sucking gently and massaging his sac with her hand. With the other hand, she dug her fingernails into his buttock and heard his hissed *"Yes!"* His obvious enjoyment made her heart soar, and when he drew away and pushed her back onto the bed, his cock was almost straining, engorged, and rock-hard.

Enda crushed his mouth against hers as he hitched her legs around his waist. "Are you ready for me, baby?"

Ama gave a frustrated moan, and he laughed before launching his cock into her and ramming his hips against hers. Ama gave a cry of intense release and clung to him as he fucked her, her fingernails digging into the toned muscles of his back. "God, Enda ...*yes* ...harder ...*harder* ..."

He obliged, laughing, and kissed her passionately. She was utterly lost in this man's arms, completely at the mercy of his body and his desire for her ...Jesus, his cock was incredible, and she was amazed she was able to take him in so deeply. She clung to him, wanting to savor every moment of his skin against hers, his mouth hungrily kissing hers, and the clean scent of him.

She came again, hard, and Enda reached his climax, pumping cum deep inside her. She didn't want him to pull away at first, and so, for a few minutes, he stayed inside her, kissing her tenderly. *"Bella Ama,"* he whispered in that deep, sensual voice, and Ama sighed happily.

Finally, he lay at her side, propped up on his elbow, gazing down at her. His hand traced a path down her body, his long, warm fingers splaying over her belly. "Ama? May I ask you something?"

Ama smiled up at him. "Anything."

"Before your wedding ...had you ever made love?"

She gave a half-embarrassed chuckle. "Is it that obvious? No, I hadn't, Enda. I was a virgin."

"It surprises me ...and to answer your question—no, it's not obvi-ous. At all. Just a hunch on my part. You are an incredible lover, my darling."

My darling. The words thrilled her. She stroked his face. "About the wedding ...Enda, you saved that day for me. I was so miserable, but when I saw you in the church ...god, I have never felt like that before."

Enda smiled. "Me either, although my reputation would probably contradict that."

Ama grinned. "Luckily, I knew very little about you. I *know* very little about you. I'm looking forward to getting to know you." She sighed. "If I had met you before ...well, it wasn't even as if I had a choice in marrying Jackson."

Enda nuzzled his nose to hers. "I know. Olivier told me the reason. I think you are a selfless person."

"Sometimes I can't believe this is modern times," she muttered, half to herself.

Enda studied her. "Ama ...why were you a virgin? Can I ask, or is that too personal?"

She smiled at him. "Like I said, you can ask me anything. The reason is ...I know it's modern thinking to just enjoy yourself and sleep with anyone and that's an absolutely fine way to live. It just wasn't for me. Before now, I was completely focused on my work."

"I would love to hear you play sometime."

She kissed him. "And so you shall. We have a recital coming up at the end of the month, at the conservatory."

"I'll be there." He moved his body on top of her. "When do you have to be back at work this afternoon?"

Ama grinned, wrapping her legs around his waist. "Not for an hour or two."

"Hmm," he grinned and plunged his cock into her. "What shall we do for an hour or two?"

Ama moaned as he thrust harder and harder until she was screaming his name.

LENA EYED HER. "Why are you glowing?"

Ama, knowing that the multiple orgasms that Enda had given her were the reason, shrugged. "Just having a good day."

She went into her office and slid the burner phone from her purse into her desk. In the small bathroom attached to her office, she looked in the mirror and saw her eyes shining. Her skin indeed was glowing. *You look like a woman who's been thoroughly and expertly fucked.*

Enda Gallo. My lover. She kept saying it to herself over and over as she worked, and when she went to teach her class that afternoon, her good mood infected her students and she had a blast with them.

Driving home, though, the usual dread set in. She could barely stand to be in the same room as Jackson, and it was with relief that she saw Olivier's car in the driveway.

She was smiling when she went in, still lost in her memories of the afternoon, and distracted. She didn't see Jackson approach her until he crushed his lips against hers. Horrified, she pushed him away. "Take your hands off me."

Jackson was unrepentant, grasping her upper arm.

"Come. We have a visitor."

Olivier stood and hugged her. She deliberately made a fuss of him to annoy Jackson and was rewarded with a glare from her husband.

"This is a nice surprise ...you'll stay for dinner, yes? Where's Mac?"

"Upstairs, not feeling well." Jackson's tone was dismissive.

Olivier smiled at her. "Love to stay. How are you?"

"In the four days since I saw you last?" She grinned at him. She had the feeling that his presence was for her benefit; Olivier had an air of the protective older brother about him.

OVER DINNER, a sumptuous duck dish prepared by Mac's chef, Ama and Olivier chatted easily, mostly ignoring the glowering presence of Jackson. He finally had enough of not being the center of attention.

"I hear your father's business is in trouble again," he said suddenly. Ama looked at him, her expression smooth.

"Not that I know of, but then I haven't spoken to my father in a while."

Jackson smirked. "The cash injection I gave him soon got spent. Seems your bride price wasn't enough. That's what you get for having a cheapskate dad, I suppose."

"Jackson," Olivier's tone was harsh. "That's enough."

Ama was staring at Jackson with undisguised disgust. "And, yet, my *'bride price'* wasn't enough to allow you everything you wanted, was it?"

Jackson's smile faded, and Ama realized he'd probably been boasting about his conquest of her to his brothers. For a moment, she regretted saying anything. Olivier looked uncomfortable.

Ama took a slug of wine and tried to ease the atmosphere. "Listen, we are having a recital at the conservatory at the end of the month. Would you like to come, Olly? Bring a date?"

Olivier nodded. "I would love to ...are you playing?"

She nodded. "Although, I'm very rusty. I need to practice more than I have been. It's hard to find the time with work being so hectic."

"We should get you a piano here," Jackson said suddenly. "Then you could practice here, and maybe I could see more of you."

Ama didn't know how to respond to that. Was he being friendly or setting a trap for her?

"That might be a solution," she said carefully. Jackson gave a nod. "Consider it done."

Ama exchanged a glance with Olivier. She hated that every conversation she had with her husband was loaded, making her feel tense and jumpy. She closed her eyes and rubbed the bridge of her nose.

"You okay?" Olivier, of course, was the one asking, and she smiled at him.

"Just tired." *From fucking your glorious half-brother*, she wanted to scream at Jackson, but then she felt remorse. Maybe her own attitude wasn't helping the marriage. She wasn't going to go soft on him ...but she could make an effort to be friendlier. Was she so scared of leading him on?

Yes.

The thought of Jackson making love to her made her want to vomit. He had bought her, for chrissakes. That wasn't love. That was possession. Ama felt sick and pushed her chair back.

"Forgive me, Olivier ...Jackson. I really am tired. I think I'd better go lie down. Will you excuse me?"

"Of course." Olivier stood as she got up and kissed her cheek. "Get some rest, honey."

She smiled at him gratefully and thought, *if I weren't already falling for Enda, it would be so easy to love you, you sweetheart of a man.* She glanced at Jackson.

"Goodnight, darling," he said in an even tone. She nodded.

"Goodnight, Jackson."

THE NEXT EVENING, when she returned from work, a Bösendorfer Imperial Concert Grand piano was waiting for her in the drawing room. Ama couldn't believe it. She sat down on the stool and ran her fingers lightly over the keys.

"I hope you like it."

She turned to see Jackson in the doorway, watching her. She cleared her throat. "It's too much."

"No."

He walked over and pulled up a chair next to her. "Ama ...we have gotten off on the wrong foot. I know you don't love me, and I'm not saying that I'm in love with you. But I want the chance to be. At least the chance to see if we can make this work. I'm not under any illusion that you won't file for divorce the moment the contract is up. But maybe we could enjoy these two years."

Ama considered his words. "Jackson ...I don't want to live in a house of misery, where I'm afraid to sleep with my door unlocked. Let's get one thing straight. I will never, ever sleep with you. *Ever.* But if we can put that aside and tolerate that ...we could try to be friends. Companions. If you need sex, feel free to look around. There are plenty of open marriages."

Careful now, she told herself, *don't give him any reason to suspect you. Just because your brain is still frazzled from having Enda Gallo's cock buried deep in you this afternoon ...careful.*

Jackson's expression was carefully composed. "Fine." He got up and walked away from her, and she sighed. The house was too quiet tonight. She went to her room and locked the door behind her. Had she done the right thing? Or had she aroused his suspicions, which would make sneaking off to the apartment much harder?

Ama reached into her purse and pulled out the burner phone. She had been about to put it on her desk at work before she left, but something told her to take it home. She wanted to know that she could talk to Enda whenever she wanted. That she could hear his voice. This afternoon she had spent another blissful hour in his arms, but they didn't have time to actually talk or to find out about each other in the stolen moments they spent. Not that she was complaining ...her lover had ravished her body, leaving her shivering with pleasure.

She smiled at the memory and went to draw a bath.

ENDA GALLO WENT BACK to his hotel. He knew he could stay at the apartment he had rented, but every time he went there increased the chances he would be recognized and that his cover would be blown.

And, besides, without Ama in his arms, the place seemed lonely, echoing with the memory of her. At least at the hotel he could distract himself and get some work done. Back in Italy, his property business had taken him years to build, but now he was about to form a partnership with his friend, Raffaelo Winter, to open a chain of boutique hotels around the world.

He called Raffaelo at home in Naples now. It was eight a.m. in Italy, and Raffaelo picked up straight away.

"Ciao, Raff."

"Hey, *ciao*, my friend." Raffaelo sounded relaxed, and Enda guessed that he must be at home with Inca, his gorgeous wife of almost ten years. Enda had met Inca soon after she and Raff had become engaged and had been devastated when she had been stabbed by a jealous stalker. Enda had tried to be there for Raff as much as he could during her recovery and the time they had spent together had only strengthened their bond. People remarked on their physical similarities, but Enda had laughed off the suggestion they could be related. His mother, his dear mother, had passed away only recently, and it was due to Raff and Inca—and Raff's twin brother, Tommaso—that he hadn't felt entirely alone in Italy.

He chatted easily with his friend now before Raffaelo told him his news. "We're coming to the States soon. Inca wants to visit her friend, Olly, in Seattle, so we thought we'd do that and then come down to SF. Sound good?"

Enda was overjoyed. "God, man, yes. How soon can you come?"

Raff laughed. "That bad, eh? Well, we're flying to Seattle this Friday, staying for a week, and then down to you. So, ten days? We don't have any restriction on time, so we can stay as long as we're welcome. Bo is performing at Pride, then doing a couple of nights at the Fillmore, so Tommaso and their vast brood will be there too."

Enda grinned. Tommaso had fallen in love with singing superstar Bo Kennedy at Raffaelo and Inca's wedding—or just after—and between them, they now had seven kids: five of their own, Matteo, Tommaso's son, and Tiger, Bo's teenage boy, both from previous relationships. They divided their time between Italy and the United Kingdom and so they were rarely in the US.

Suddenly Enda wanted to tell Raffaelo about Ama—about how much he cared for her and thought about her all of the time. He so desperately wanted to introduce her to his friends. Maybe there was a way ...

"Hey listen, before you go, I wanted to float an idea to you. I know we said on the next project we would concentrate on hotels, but how about we look into building music schools for the less privileged? Jackson's new wife," he almost choked on those words, "Amalia, is a classical pianist and tutor, and she got me thinking maybe there's a new outlet." He knew he was rambling now. "Anyway, just something to think about."

"Of course. I like the idea of that. Let's talk when I'm in town. Maybe we should meet Amalia."

Enda punched the air silently, grinning. "Definitely."

When he had ended the call, Enda went to shower, then got into bed. What he would give to take Ama to meet his friends as his partner. *Two years,* he said to himself. *Two years and she'll be free, and then I'm going to marry that girl.*

The thought brought him up short. *Marriage? Wow.* Marriage had never been something he had aspired to or wanted, but with her ... with Ama ... *well, damn.*

His phone bleeped, and it was with delighted pleasure that he recognized the number as Ama's burner phone.

Missing you. Thinking only of you.

Enda smiled and tapped out a reply.

I wish you were with me right now, Bella.

Me too, gorgeous. Sleep well.

ENDA BROUGHT up the subject of the music schools at dinner with his family, careful not to give away that he and Ama had already discussed it earlier that day, when they had spent a blissful afternoon in his apartment, screwing each other senseless and talking. They were learning so much about each other in those precious hours. Enda discovered that, despite her great beauty, Ama hated to be judged on that, and preferred to be complimented on her brain or her humor. That underneath her almost regal presence, she was, at heart, a book nerd, an art lover, and someone who declared she would be unable to live without music. Not just classical, either, but rock, and cheesy pop songs—and Johnny Cash.

Enda found himself opening up to her about his family—or lack of it—until Olivier came to find him. "I never knew they existed," he admitted, and then grinned at her. "And in the end, I got the best and the worst of brothers. I love Olivier. He gave me a way to know my father, and he's been nothing but supportive. I even suspect if he had known about us, that he would have been our biggest cheerleader."

Ama smiled at him. "I was thinking the same thing, actually. Still, I don't think it's a good idea to clue him in. I would hate to put him in an awkward position."

"Agreed."

So, now, as they all sat around Macaulay Gallo's vast dinner table, Enda made sure he didn't make eye-contact with Ama when he told them his and Raff's ideas.

Jackson made a scoffing noise. "Really? Where's the profit in that?"

Enda looked at him coolly. "I would think, in your position, that you would see that money isn't everything. How many more billions do you need, Jackson? Isn't it time you gave something back?"

"Didn't I just broker the deal that saved Amalia's sister from an abusive marriage?" Jackson grinned at his wife, who stared back in dislike.

"I don't think that's what Enda meant," she said softly. She turned to her lover and tried not to show in her face how much she felt for him, "I think it's a wonderful idea. Schools all over the country are having their funding for the arts cut to almost nothing. They're forcing the kids to focus on science and math and disregarding the kids who were born to be artists, actors, musicians. It's just wrong."

Enda smiled at her. "Maybe you should come along, meet Raffaelo, and be our consultant on the inside."

"Love to." Ama hid a grin, obviously realizing what he was up to, but Jackson cleared his throat.

"I don't see why that would help."

Ama turned cold eyes on him. "I wasn't asking your permission."

Enda saw the anger in Jackson's eyes. His father did too, apparently, because Mac changed the subject hurriedly. "Jackson, I was going to ask you. I got a call today from that interior designer you told me about. She was under the impression that you have arranged for some work to be done."

Jackson nodded. "I have. All of the bedrooms, except yours, Dad, because I know you've just had it remodeled."

"Excuse me?" Amalia looked bemused. "*All* of the bedrooms?"

Jackson nodded, his smile smug. "Yes, darling, all of them. I thought we could take a penthouse at a hotel while the work is being done."

Ama flushed angrily, and Enda narrowed his eyes at his brother. He was trying to force her to share his bed. *Asshole.* Ama picked up her wine and sipped it casually. "A single room will be okay with me. Or I can stay with a friend."

There it was. In the open. With those simple words, Ama had outed the sham of her marriage to both Olivier and Macaulay. If she had shouted, 'I'm not sleeping with Jackson,' at the top of her voice, it couldn't be more obvious. Enda watched Jackson's face turned from red to purple and suddenly felt afraid for Ama. He knew of old what Jackson's temper was like.

PENELOPE ...three years ago, she had borne the brunt of Jackson's temper and what had happened had scarred everyone ...

2

___

PART TWO

Three years ago ...

E nda took a slug of whiskey and turned back to the party. He hated these things, but his father, Macaulay Gallo, who he couldn't get used to calling 'dad' yet, had insisted.

"If you want to be part of this family, Enda, you must see how we operate."

He had meant it kindly, but it struck at the heart of Enda's misgivings. He hadn't yet decided that he wanted to be part of this family. It had been four years ago when Olivier had found him, and since then, he had grown close to his older brother, but his father was still distant. The youngest Gallo son, Jackson ...Enda had loathed him on sight.

He looked over to him now and saw him standing with his girlfriend, Penelope. They were obviously having some sort of argument, Jackson berating his girlfriend for some slight he perceived she had made.

Penelope was a lovely young woman. With caramel-colored hair and dark blue eyes, she was the head of a local charity. Her family was old money, but Penelope worked tirelessly to help others. What the hell she was doing with Jackson, Enda had no clue.

IT WAS TWO DAYS LATER, in the city, that Enda had seen her meeting with another man. From the delight on his face—and hers—they were obviously in love. Enda was glad. Penny looked radiant as she talked with the man. *Good,* Enda thought. *Jackson can go fuck himself. You go for it, Penny.* He had intended to just walk away, but she suddenly spotted him and the color drained from her face. Enda cursed to himself, then walked over.

"Hey, Penny. Hey there, I'm Enda Gallo." he smiled at her companion and shook his hand.

"Danny McNamara. Would you like to join us?" The young man looked uncomfortable. Enda hesitated, looking at Penny. He didn't want to be rude. Penny nodded tightly.

"Just for a minute, then I have to be going."

They sat, and Penny explained who Enda was. The young man, Danny, nodded.

Enda couldn't bear the tension. "Look, I just wanted to say. I'm glad. You both look so happy. Hell, I'm *delighted* for you, Penny. You have my word; Jackson will not hear of this from me. *Fuck* him."

Danny looked relieved and Penny looked close to tears. She put her hand on his arm.

"Thank you, Enda." She sighed, wiping away her tears. "I tried to finish it with Jackson ...he won't accept it. He just cuts me off. I can't do it anymore, Enda. He's ...abusive. He cheats constantly. And he ..." She broke off and shook her head. Enda and Danny exchanged a concerned glance. Penny didn't have to say anymore. That Jackson beat her was obvious.

"You don't have to worry about it anymore, Pen," Danny said.

Enda nodded. "Is there somewhere you can stay while he gets the message?"

Penny nodded, looking over at Danny. "We've just bought an apartment in Palo Alto. He'll have no clue we're there."

A WEEK LATER, Penny had called Enda in hysterics. "It's Danny. He was in a hit-and-run. Oh god, oh god, they've taken him to the hospital, but it's bad, Enda, so bad. I know it was Jackson ...please, can you come?"

He raced to the hospital, but it was too late. Danny was pronounced dead on arrival, and Enda had to help a hysterical Penny while processing his own shock. Was Jackson really capable of murder? He didn't want to believe it, but something in his half-brother's make up made him think he would be. A month later, his worst fears were realized.

A still-grieving Penny left her office just after eight p.m. and went down to the parking garage. She got into her Mercedes and was distracted by her phone ringing. She smiled when she saw who was calling.

"Hey, Enda, how are you?"

"I'm okay, sweetheart. I was just thinking about you. How're things?"

"I ..."

Penny never got to tell him. From her backseat, a masked attacker pounced, one arm curling around her neck. When she grabbed at his arm to try and prize it free, he drove a knife into her stomach again and again. Penny screamed until she could no longer breathe when the blood loss and shock grew too much. Her killer was savage and merciless, stabbing her again and again until she slumped in the seat. In her last moments, she could hear Enda screaming her name and the final whisper of her killer.

"Jackson Gallo wants you to know—*nobody* leaves him."

With a last thrust of the knife, he stabbed Penny in the heart and ended her life.

· · ·

ENDA WOULD NEVER FORGET that night. The sound of a defenseless woman being brutally murdered ...and the worst thing was, in the midst of it, Jackson had walked into the room where Enda was with a triumphant look on his face, and Enda knew, for sure, his half-brother was a murderer. Enda flew across the room and punched him, the brothers rolling around until Olivier pulled Enda off Jackson. Enda stormed out of the room, calling the police as he got into his car and sped to Penny's office. He got there just as the police arrived. He would never forget the sight of Penny, slumped in the driver's seat, covered in blood. She had been butchered. That much was obvious. Enda had no compunction in telling the police everything he had heard and that he thought Jackson was behind the murder.

JACKSON WAS QUESTIONED about Penny's murder, but never arrested or charged. There was simply no evidence against him. Penny was buried, at her request, next to Danny, but at her funeral Jackson played the part of the grieving boyfriend perfectly. Staggered by the lack of justice wrought by Jackson's position and billions, Enda was repelled by him and had left the country. He'd stayed away from his family since then—even Olivier, who he adored. Olivier had finally flown to Italy to plead with him not to abandon him and Mac, just because of Jackson. It had taken some persuasion, but finally, Enda agreed. When Olivier told him, a few years later, that Jackson was marrying Amalia, Enda couldn't help but feel a chill go down his spine.

When he found out the circumstances of the marriage, the arrangement, and the coercion of Amalia Rai to marry Jackson, Enda had felt the shock keenly. Enda determined then to go to the wedding and make sure that the signs weren't there—that Jackson had finally fallen in love for real.

He had been disappointed, but not shocked, when he saw in his younger half-brother the same possessive contempt that he had shown Penny. Amalia was there to be his property. Enda was pleased to see that Amalia hadn't been as subservient as Jackson would like, even on her wedding day. And when he, Enda, had made love to the beautiful bride in the garden just hours later, he'd seen her strength.

He just hoped it was enough to save her life.

AMA WAS RELIEVED when Olivier accompanied them home. "I just want to talk to dad for a while," he said, but she knew he was there to keep the peace, at least until Jackson calmed down. Enda had been desperate to do the same, but she had shaken her head at him. *I don't want him to guess*, she tried to communicate with her look, and she thought Enda had gotten it. God, she was crazy about that man, though. She would call him later, when it was safe.

She went to her room as soon as she got home and began to run a bath. Going back into her room, she checked the door was locked, then propped her usual chair underneath the handle. *God, what a way to live.* But Jackson scared her. There was violence in him, she was sure, and it wasn't far from the surface—ever. Ama knew Olivier and Enda thought so too.

She stripped off and sank into the tub, feeling the soothing water ease her aching body. She ached from tension constantly now. The only time she ever relaxed was with Enda, naked and gasping for air in his arms. *God, that man ...*

She slipped her hand between her legs and began to rub, thinking about the last time they'd made love. It had been a slow, leisurely afternoon of making love, Enda cradling her in his arms as his cock plowed deep inside her. God, would she ever get tired of this? He had flipped her onto her stomach, parted her buttocks gently, then asked if she was sure. She had nodded, and he had eased into her ass, his other hand stroking her clit. She'd come almost violently, surprising herself. When he'd wrapped his tie around her wrists and fucked her, holding her hostage to him and his huge cock. She'd loved every moment of being dominated by him. Even when she was straddling him, he was in charge, impaling her on his cock, gripping her hips with strong fingers, and cumming on her belly and breasts.

Amalia could hardly bring herself to leave him every day, and she fantasized now about going home to him in the evening. About opening the front door, only to be greeted by his fierce kiss, his hands pushing up her skirt, and his cock thrusting into her as he fucked her hard against the wall.

Ama gave a soft moan as she stroked and dreamed her way to an orgasm. Relaxing afterward, she wondered if she could call him later and maybe indulge in some phone sex.

That man has turned you into a nympho, she grinned to herself. *God, I love you, Enda Gallo.*

Her eyes flew open and she gasped in shock. Oh god ...she *did* love him. She was *completely* in love with the man.

"Shit," she said and got out of the bath. Love complicated everything, and it made her uneasy. What if she couldn't hide it much longer? What would Jackson do?

And she didn't want to risk Enda's position in the family. From what he had told her, he had loved being a part of it, for Olivier's sake at least. The two Gallo's she loved with her whole heart would be hurt and she couldn't stand that.

She dried herself, wrapped the towel around her, and went back into her bedroom to dry her hair. She was lost in thought as she grabbed her brush.

"Nice show you gave me there."

Ama gasped and whirled around. Jackson was leaning against her door, smiling nastily. Ama reddened at the thought of him watching her masturbate.

"What the fuck are you doing in my room, asshole?"

Jackson smiled, then in a flash, he had her by her throat. "Watch what you call me, *wife*. I've had just about enough of your insubordination."

Ama kicked out at him, struggling to get free. He clamped a hand over her mouth.

"Ssh, ssh ..." He lay on top of her. He took out his phone and showed her a picture. "Do you recognize this apartment?"

Ama went cold. "It's my sister's place."

"That's right. Now, this photo was taken, oh, about three minutes ago. Your sister's alone there right now."

Ama stopped struggling. "What the hell do you think you're doing?"

Jackson grinned and kissed her, grinding his mouth down on hers. Ama tasted blood. "One of the two Rai sisters is getting fucked tonight, Amalia. It's up to you which one."

Ama's horror was overwhelming. "You bastard ...you leave her alone, you fucking *bastard*."

Jackson grinned. "That sounds like a decision to me."

He yanked her towel away, admiring her naked body. "God, it's about time I got to see the goods. You're so fucking sexy ..."

He was unzipping his fly now and Amalia started to cry. Would he really have Selima raped if Ama didn't sleep with him?

Yes. You know he would. Oh my god ...

Jackson pushed her legs apart and thrust into her, and Ama cried out. Jackson clamped his hand over her mouth again. "Now listen to me, whore. I'm going to fuck you every night of our marriage, and you'll let me, or I swear to god, I will hurt everyone you care about. Everyone. And I'll finish with you, Amalia. I swear to god. And if you ever leave me? I'll *kill* you. I'll rip you apart."

He continued to thrust as silent tears poured down Ama's cheeks. She closed her eyes as he pumped away, his cock shooting thin streams of cum inside her. *No. No, this cannot be happening.*

He pulled out, satisfied. "Guess I got the worth of the bride price now."

Ama curled up in a ball and sobbed. Jackson chuckled. "Get used to it, little girl. I mean it when I say I'll destroy you if you tell anyone about this. *Anyone*."

And then he was gone.

Ama stayed curled up on the counterpane, shocked to her core about what had just happened. Rape. Jackson had raped her. He'd threatened to have her family attacked and threatened to kill her.

How the hell was she ever going to survive this marriage? Her burner phone vibrated in her nightstand drawer, but she couldn't face talking to Enda—not to the man she loved when the man she despised had just done this to her.

Ama wanted nothing more than to go to sleep and never wake up.

RAFFAELO WINTER BEAR-HUGGED his good friend Enda as soon as Enda saw them alight from the private plane. Inca, Raffaelo's exquisite wife, was grinning and rolling her eyes at them. Enda laughed as Raffaelo released him and he embraced Inca.

"Hello, gorgeous. Still married to this wretch, then?"

Inca smiled at him. She had stunning eyes, he thought, warm and loving, and her face was perfection. Her long, dark hair was caught up in a ponytail, and she was adorably scruffy in t-shirt and jeans. Enda was hit with the thought that she and Ama would have a lot in common. Both Indian-American, both gorgeous talented and funny.

They chatted as they drove in Enda's limousine from Raffaelo's private jet, and Enda marveled at the easy love between Raff and Inca. They had been through hell together, but were still as in love as ever. Raffaelo, his dark curls now cropped close to his head and flecked with silver, sported a beard which made him look, according to Inca, like a 'sexy grumpy professor.'"

"And who knew my kink was sexy, grumpy professors?" she joked, and Raffaelo ran a finger down her cheek, grinning.

Enda felt a spark of envy. How he would love to have this open, joking, fun relationship with Ama, but over the last week, she had been subdued and withdrawn. She told him she was just tired, but even though they had known each other for such a short time, he knew she was holding something back from him. When they made love, she clung to him as if she wanted to never let go, but it was tinged with a quiet desperation.

Today, though, she would meet up with him and his friends in public, ostensibly to discuss the music school idea, but really, Enda hoped, just to bond with his friends. The music schools would provide good cover for Ama meet up with him and Raff, and if she and Inca were to become friends ...

"Hey, Enda? You in there? When are we meeting Amalia?"

Enda checked his watch. "Are you sure you don't want to go back to the hotel and get some sleep? We're not due to meet her until one."

Inca colored slightly. "We, um, slept on the plane." She and Raff exchanged a conspiratorial grin, and once again, Enda felt a pang of loneliness.

As THEY WERE SEATED at the restaurant, Enda looked up to see Amalia entering and speaking to the maître d', then glancing over to him. Her face lit up when she saw him and he stood to greet her.

"*Ciao*, Ama. Great to see you." It felt weird to kiss her on the cheek, rather than taste her sweet mouth. She looked beautiful, but he could see dark violet circles under her eyes, and she looked like she had lost some weight. Her cheeks were slightly hollowed, and there was an air of sadness around her. What the hell was going on?

Enda introduced her to Raffaelo and Inca, the latter of whom hugged the other woman. "It's so good to meet you."

Ama smiled at her. "And you. I've heard so much about you both. And, damn, Raff, you and Enda could be twins."

Raffaelo grinned. "I already have one of those, but I know what you mean. Good to meet you, Ama."

Enda wanted so badly to hold Ama's hand as they sat together; he had to be satisfied with just sitting by her, breathing in her perfume.

Inca grinned at him, and he realized she had guessed exactly what Ama meant to him. He was glad. The four of them chatted easily throughout dinner. Inca and Raff told them they were contemplating adoption, but at the same time, enjoyed their independence.

"I love having Tommaso and Bo's kids to stay, but when they go home, I have to admit, I'm exhausted. So ...we don't know. Maybe kids aren't for us," Inca shrugged and smiled at her husband.

"Maybe not," he agreed and laughed. "It would be harder for us to go on one of our adventures."

Inca told Ama about their penchant for travel. "We went to Peru last year, hiked up to Machu Picchu, and went to the Convento de San Francisco Ossuary."

"That was creepy. Entirely made out of human bones." Raff shuddered, but Inca grinned.

"I loved it. The worst was that rope bridge you made me walk across. God."

"Wuss."

Inca play-punched his shoulder. "The words 'hand-woven' and 'bridge' should never go together."

Enda, watching how easy and playful his friend's relationship was, couldn't help but slide his hand along Ama's thigh. She started, dropping her fork, which slid from the table. "Oops, sorry."

She bent over to retrieve it, and her shirt rode up, revealing a strip of creamy, golden skin ...and the very definite imprint of a boot, bruised into the skin of her side and stomach. Enda's breath caught in his throat and Inca, who had seen it too, met his gaze in alarm.

Jackson. The bastard. The fury burned in Enda's throat, and when Ama sat up, tugging her shirt down and flushing, he saw her reaction to his confusion.

Lunch was subdued after that. Raffaelo seemed a little confused by the sadness that had come over the other three, and when Enda and Ama said goodbye, he hugged his friend.

"We will get together soon, yes?"

Enda nodded, not trusting himself to speak. The two men watched the women hug, and Inca whispered something to Ama, who nodded, tears in her eyes.

ENDA TOOK an un-protesting Ama back to his apartment and poured them both a whiskey. As she sipped, he lifted her shirt and studied the horrendous pattern of bruises on her stomach, back and sides.

"He did this."

She nodded, looking shattered. "Yes."

"That's it. I've had it. I don't care about anyone else but you. You need to leave that house tonight."

"No."

"No?" Enda was astonished.

"I can't. He ...he'll hurt people. People I care about."

"He's hurting you!"

"I can take it."

Enda lost it then. "How can you be so blind? You're an intelligent, brave woman and he's reducing you to what? His punching bag? Is he doing anything ...?" He only got part way through the question before he realized. "Oh, dear god ...is he raping you?"

Ama gave a sob and nodded. Enda took her in his arms. He wanted to kill Jackson right there, right then. "What's he holding over you, baby? What is it?"

She told him and he closed his eyes. He had no trouble believing Jackson would have Selima or anyone else Ama loved hurt or even killed. He could understand how Ama thought she was backed into a corner. Bastard.

Enda sat down with her on his couch. "Ama, I know you want to protect your sister. I do. But I think there's something you need to understand about Jackson. He's ...psychopathic. My father won't hear it, and Olivier struggles with accepting it even though he knows it's the truth. Has Olly told you about Penelope?"

Ama shook her head, looking desolate and exhausted. "No."

Enda took a deep breath in. "Penny was Jackson's girlfriend, of sorts, a few years back. They didn't date for long; Penny could see what kind of man he was. So, she tried to end it. Jackson, of course, is never dumped. By anyone. When Penny met someone else, Danny, Jackson had them both murdered. Danny by a hit-and-run driver. Penny was stabbed to death in her car."

Ama looked as if she was going to throw up. "*Jesus. Jesus.*" She bent double, wrapping her arms around herself. When she looked up at Enda, tears were flooding down her face. "What if he does the same to Selima?" Her voice was barely a whisper. "I might leave him, but what if he has her killed before I'm even down the driveway? At the very least, he'll destroy my father's business."

"Inca saw the bruises too. What did she say to you?"

Ama smiled through her tears. "She told me all I had to do was ask and she'll be there for me. I love her already."

Enda took her in his arms. "I'm so scared for you, baby," he said softly. "I swear, we will find a way out of this."

Ama nodded, pressing her lips against his. "I don't want to go home, just for tonight. I'll tell him our meeting with Inca and Raff went late, so I decided to stay in the city with friends."

Enda kissed her back. "*Cara mia*, I want to make you happy again."

AMA PULLED AWAY from him and stood, pulling her shirt over her head and slipping out of her skirt. Enda pressed his lips to her belly, careful not to hurt her bruises. Jackson certainly knew where to beat someone so that it wouldn't show. *Fucker.*

With a rush of adrenaline, Enda swept her into his arms and carried her to bed. Ama gazed up at him as he stripped. "Don't wait, my darling. Don't wait."

His cock, already ramrod hard and bobbing under its own weight, entered her and she shivered with pleasure as her cunt tightened around it. They fit together so perfectly it almost seemed unbelievable. They made love slowly and intensely until both came, shivering through a mellow orgasm. Enda kissed her tenderly.

"I'm not hurting you, am I?"

Ama shook her head and tried to smile. "No. You're erasing bad memories, if that helps."

To his surprise, Enda found tears in his own eyes. "I hate this. I hate what he is doing to you."

Ama nodded, clinging to him. "I know. But I have to protect my family. Until I can figure out a way ..."

There was a furious pounding on the front door of the apartment and they both froze. Nobody knew they were there or even knew Enda owned the penthouse. Enda sat up and wrapped the sheet around Ama. "Go into the bathroom and stay there. Keep the light off."

She nodded and disappeared into the dark room. Enda got up and tugged his jeans on as the knocking came again.

Steeling himself, he tugged open the door. Olivier stood outside and Enda gaped at him. "Olly ...what the hell?"

Olivier shook his head. "No time for explanations now. It's dad, Enda. He's had a massive heart attack. He's in the hospital." Olivier looked devastated and scared. "Bring Ama. We'll tell Jackson we picked her up on the way."

As THEY ALL three ran the corridors of the hospital, a million questions whirled around Ama's brain. So, Olivier knew about her and Enda and knew about the apartment. How the hell did he know? She couldn't think of a way that wasn't negative. And that's what was killing her—thinking bad things about Olivier, whom she adored, as she knew Enda did. She trusted—had trusted—Olivier with her life. And now ...

They saw Jackson up ahead, and for once, Ama felt sorry for the monster. At this moment, he looked like the lost little boy, rather than the scheming rapist and possible murderer she now thought of him as. This was a different Jackson—vulnerable. She patted his arm awkwardly. "I'm so sorry, Jackson."

He looked right through her, ignoring Enda entirely and looked in desperation at his older brother. "They won't tell me anything, Olly."

Olivier nodded, his face grim. "They're probably still trying to do what they do, Jack. Let's go sit together and wait."

Ama couldn't bring herself to sit with Jackson, so she sat opposite him. She caught Olivier's eye, and he smiled kindly. She felt a rush of relief that he wasn't judging her for sleeping with Enda. Enda sat next to her, his arm across the back of her chair, and it was so tempting to just snuggle into him. He looked shocked, but grim-faced, and Ama could tell he was trying to keep it together.

An hour later, the doctor came to see them. "I'm Dr. Friedan. I'm the chief of cardiology here," she said and gave them a warm smile. "Mr. Gallo suffered a severe heart attack, as you know. Now, we've managed to stabilize him, but the next twenty-four hours are critical."

"Can we see him?"

Dr. Friedan shook her head. "I'd rather you didn't for a few hours. Let him rest. He regained consciousness briefly, but he's sleeping now. Come back in the morning."

After she'd gone, Jackson slumped in his chair. "I'm not leaving."

Olivier looked at Enda. "Maybe you should take Ama home and stay with her at the house until we have some news."

Ama looked at Jackson, who hadn't even seemed to hear Olivier. "We should go."

AT MACAULAY GALLO'S HOME, the place rang with emptiness. Ama didn't want to sleep or go to the room where Jackson had been abusing her all week, so she and Enda made camp in the large kitchen. There was a large, well-worn couch and they sat there together, watching dawn break outside the window.

"You know, it's funny," Enda said quietly, "Even now, I can't think of him as my father. I know the DNA tests said he was—sorry, *is,* but ...it's Olivier I stayed for. If it had just been Mac and Jackson, then maybe I would have not been so involved with the family." He smiled sadly at her. "But then I wouldn't have met you, *amore mia.*"

Ama stroked his cheek. "So we have to talk about the fact that Olivier knows about us."

"It would seem."

They sat in silence, contemplating what that meant. Enda gave up. "I just can't figure it out. We were so careful."

Ama was chewing her lip. "Do you think Jackson knows?"

He shook his head. "No. Because if he did ..."

He didn't have to finish the sentence. Ama knew he meant that if

Jackson knew, they'd both probably be dead right now. Ama's mind went back to what Enda had told her about Penelope. Ama had no problem imagining Jackson stabbing *her* to death for sleeping with Enda. She tamped down the terror. Better her than Enda …or Selima, but she didn't say that out loud.

Just after seven a.m., she finally fell asleep, wrapped in Enda's arms as they lay on the couch together.

At eight a.m. Olivier called them to tell them Macaulay was dead.

The funeral was attended by hundreds of people. Inca and Raffaelo came too, sad-eyed, hugging Enda and Olivier. Ama dutifully took Jackson's arm as they followed the casket into the church and sat with him as the service began. Jackson seemed out of it, and Ama wondered to Enda if he had taken something to get through it all.

Macaulay's death had hit him hard. Gone was the hubris and posturing; Jackson was grieving. Even Enda had felt sorry for the – man—as much as he could. He couldn't shake the anger he felt towards Jackson over his treatment of Ama—the threats to her family if she didn't comply with him. He studied them as a couple now; Jackson's perfectly coiffed hair and cleanly shaven face, next to Ama's ethereal, sad beauty. *No.* They made no sense as a couple. Why was Jackson so entirely set on pretending they were?

Enda was plagued with nightmares about Ama being murdered by one of Jackson's goons. He pictured her in her car, gutted, blood everywhere…*Jesus, man, stop it.* He bent his head, closing his eyes to erase the images. He felt Raff's hand on his shoulder and smiled at his friend gratefully.

AT THE WAKE, Ama stayed with Jackson for a time, then excused herself. She felt exhausted, drawn, and numb. She had liked Macaulay a lot, even though he was a weak man, and now that he'd gone…god, she would be alone in this house with Jackson. God knows what he would do to her when no one was there to stop him. She went to her room to change out of the formal black suit she had worn to the church and into a simple, but comfortable, black dress. She heard a soft knock on the door.

"Come in."

Inca poked her head around the door and Ama sighed with relief. "Come in, please. I need some girl time."

Inca hugged her. "It's awful. I'm so sorry." She perched on the end of Ama's bed and studied her. "How are you? Really?"

Scared. That was the first thing that flew into her mind, but she bit it back. "Okay. Sad. He was a nice old coot."

Inca smiled. "He was. And sometimes, he had good DNA."

Ama chuckled. "Yes, *sometimes.*"

Inca lowered her voice. "Ama, you can tell me anything. It's pretty obvious, to Raff and me at least, that you and Enda are together. I don't blame you, or judge you, except to say ...*yay.* Selfishly, I want my friend Enda to be happy, and it's clear to me that you are the person for him."

Ama wanted to cry. It was such a relief to be able to be honest with someone about her feelings for Enda. "It's true. It's just complicated." She told Inca about the threats Jackson had made.

Inca nodded sagely. "I get it. Look, Ama, I don't know how much Enda has told you about my past, but I had some pretty serious ... enemies, shall we say. There was a lot of violence and I nearly didn't make it. So, I'm saying ...I've dealt with the kind of things I think Jackson is threatening."

"And you made it out."

Inca nodded, her lovely face serious. "I did. And I want to help – you—we both want to help you and Enda. I don't know how, yet, but we will. Jackson has a lot of power, and now with even a third share of his father's fortune, he'll think he's untouchable."

Ama sighed. "You're right. Did you know about Penelope?"

Inca nodded. "Yes. Look, Ama, I've had some experience with obsession. It's unpredictable. I think our first step would be to secure both your and your family's safety."

"I agree. My family comes first, though. If Jackson's going to take anything out on anybody, I'd rather it was me."

Inca gave her a strange smile. "You and I are more alike than you think. I would rather die than let anything happen to Raff."

Ama smiled. "He worships you, and I expect he'd say the same."

Inca laughed. "He would. Hopefully, that part of our lives is over and done with."

Ama squeezed her hand. "And now you're on a mission to save mine."

"You betcha."

After her talk with Inca, Ama felt lighter and more positive. She rejoined the wake. People were starting to leave, and she saw Enda and Olivier talking to some of the stragglers. She moved towards them, but a hand shot out of a group of people, and Jackson hauled her to his side. The smell of alcohol coming off of him was over-powering.

"Isn't she beautiful, my wife?" He slurred and kissed her on the cheek. Ama tried to not to cringe. Macaulay's friends looked uncom-fortable, but Jackson hooked his arm around Ama's neck. "I'm a very lucky man, wouldn't you say?"

Ama tried to deflect attention by smiling politely at the elderly couple. "How are you both? You look well."

Jackson snorted. "Come on, what do you say? Arthur? Magda? Isn't Ama the most beautiful woman you ever saw? Her sister's pretty too, if you know what I mean."

God. Ama pushed him away from her. "That's enough, Jackson." She turned, red-faced, to the couple. "I'm so sorry. He's taken Mac's death really hard."

The elderly couple smiled sympathetically at her and made their escape. Soon only the family, Inca, Raff, and one other couple were left. Jackson lurched at Ama. "Don't ever contradict me again in public, bitch. That's not your job."

"That's enough, Jackson." Enda strode over and put himself between Jackson and Ama. "Go to bed and sleep it off."

Jackson sneered. "Oh, look, it's the *bastard*. Are you still here? Daddy dearest has gone now, so you can just go fuck yourself, you Italian asshole."

Enda kept his temper. "Go to bed, Jackson."

Jackson looked at Ama again and grinned nastily. "Okay. If Ama comes with me. She can suck my cock while I decide whether or not to fuck her sister too."

Ama gasped in horror, and Enda, incensed, launched himself at Jackson, landing punch after punch. Jackson staggered back against the window, smashing it, but Enda yanked him to the floor.

It took both Raffaelo and Olivier to haul Enda off the bloodied Jackson. A shocked Inca had locked her arms around a trembling and sobbing Ama and was trying to calm her down.

Jackson scrambled to his feet, wiping his mouth, and then stopped, looking between Enda and Ama. "Jesus Christ ...you're *fucking* her. *You're fucking my wife. Bastard!*"

He threw himself at Enda, but Olivier stepped between them and took the full force of Jackson's rage. They both staggered back, and it took Raffaelo to steady the pair. Olivier got his arms around his younger brother. "Stop. *Stop.*"

"You filthy Italian cocksucker," Jackson screamed at Enda, who glowered at him, "I'll fucking kill you, I'll kill *both* of you." He struggled against his brother's hold, turning his white-hot anger on Ama. "*Bitch whore.* I knew the precious princess act was fake. How long have you been opening your legs for him?"

Suddenly, Ama lost her temper. She extricated herself from Inca's arms and went to Jackson. "Do you want to know how long, Jackson? Do you really want to know? *Our wedding night*, Jackson. And do you know what else? I don't regret one moment of it because I'm in love with Enda. That's right, I *love* him. He's my world now, and you're just a bug on a windshield to me. Do you really want to me to tell them all what you do to me? How you raped me, beat me, and threatened to have my sister raped too? My father's business ruined? Fuck you, Jackson Gallo, you're not worth one billionth of Enda, or Olivier, or anyone."

There were tears pouring down her face now. "I'm leaving you and seeking an annulment. Screw you. Screw my father for doing this to Selima and me."

Jackson smiled nastily. "I'll never agree to a divorce, Amalia. Never. You belong to me."

Ama slapped his face, hard. "I don't belong to anyone, *asshole*. Remember that. I *choose* to be with Enda because I love him."

"I will ruin both of you. Both of you! Get out of my house, all of you. You," Jackson snapped at Raffaelo now. "Take your whore and get out."

Inca gave him the finger and Raffaelo smirked. "Pathetic child. Ama, how long will it take you to pack your stuff?"

"Ten minutes, tops."

Raffaelo nodded at Enda, who was still amped up, ready to kill Jackson if needed. "Go with her, Enda. We'll make sure the toddler here is occupied."

Olivier nodded at Enda, his arms still locked around Jackson, who was just grinning openly now. As Ama walked past him, he spat at her, his saliva spattering across her face. Ama merely kept walking, wiping her face, and tugging Enda with her.

Jackson stopped struggling and instead decided to stare at Inca, who regarded him coolly. His eyes ran up and down her body. Inca glanced at Raffaelo and grinned at him. He rolled his eyes.

"Is she a good fuck, Raffaelo? She looks like she's a good fuck ... nice tight little cu ..."

Inca calmly stepped up to Jackson and smashed her knee into his balls. "Quiet, *boy*," she said in a cold voice. "You're on very, *very* thin ice."

"Seconded," Raffaelo said and took Inca's hand. Olivier tried to hide a grin.

Jackson groaned, bent double with pain. "Fuckers. You have no idea what I could do to you all. None of you will get away with this."

Olivier gave an exasperated sigh. "Jackson, haven't you learned yet? You have no power here. None. Dad's gone. Ama's gone. Stop with the empty threats. Grow up."

Ama and Enda came back in, Enda pulling her suitcase. Jackson smiled at Ama. "Aren't you going to say goodbye, baby?"

Ama didn't even look at him. "Thank you, Olly. Raff. Thank you,

Inca."

And, hand-in-hand with Enda, she walked out the Gallo house forever.

Outside, he stopped her and took her in his arms. "You love me?"

"I know it's crazy fast, but, yes, Enda Gallo, I love you."

Enda grinned and kissed her. "*Ti amo*, Amalia Rai. *Ti amo*."

Three months later ...

Sorrento, Italy ...

ENDA TOOK her nipple into his mouth and Ama sighed, running her hands over his head and shoulders as he sucked and teased the tiny bud. When they were so sensitive she could scream, he moved up to kiss her and slid his huge engorged cock into her, Ama's legs wrapping themselves around his waist.

They had been living in Italy together for three months now, and it had been the happiest time in Ama's life. The villa that Raffaelo had found for them was airy and spacious, and rustic enough that Ama felt that she was really in a different world. It had wooden shutters at the windows and delicate, white voile drapes that billowed out into the rooms, giving them a dream-like quality.

When they had left San Francisco, Ama had called the dean of the conservatory, explained the situation, and asked for a sabbatical. Given the circumstances, the dean had agreed, but still, Ama felt bad about leaving them in the lurch. Enda had arranged for Selima to have a private security team, and although her sister chafed against the invasion of privacy, she had been horrified to find out what Ama had been through. Ama had tried, without success, to have her move to Italy with them, but Selima, finally free to do what she liked, had refused.

"I'm sorry, Ama, but I have a life here now. I'll take the bodyguard, but otherwise, it's business as usual. Go to Italy with your gorgeous man and be happy."

· · ·

AND AMA *WAS* HAPPY. Her father hadn't been. He screamed at her about disloyalty and dishonor until she'd had enough.

"Dad ...you pimped both of your daughters out to men who beat and raped them. Who has the dishonor?"

Her uncle, Omar, had stepped in and defended her. "Gajendra, this has gone far enough. You do not have the right."

Gajendra, his pride hurt and his business shaky, swore never to talk to his daughters again. Hurt but defiant, Amalia told him it was his loss.

"I guess we're both orphans now, baby," she told Enda, trying to put a brave face on it, but when she burst into tears, he held her tightly.

"You are my family, Amalia Rai. You, Olly, Selima, Raff, and Inca. I think myself a very lucky man."

AMA GAZED up at him now as they made love on this sultry Italian night, moving together, Enda's cock harder and deeper into her with every thrust. She felt drunk with love all the time now, and so sensual in her own femininity that she had become more adventurous in the bedroom. Enda had her hands pinned above her head, and she moaned as his pace quickened, the friction of his cock in her cunt sending shivers through her.

"I love you so much, Enda," she whispered, then gave a cry as her orgasm ripped through her. Her back arched, her belly pressing against his as she felt his cock shooting thick, creamy cum deep inside her. Enda, panting for air, kissed her, not wanting to disconnect. She squeezed her thighs around his waist. "Stay inside," she urged, and he grinned.

"If only I could forever."

Ama giggled. "Man, that would make grocery shopping awkward."

"And business meetings."

"And recitals. Here, tonight, a recital by pianist Amalia Rai, who, you will notice, will perform while being comprehensively fucked by an incredibly handsome man. Front row tickets extra."

Enda laughed out loud. "Those tickets would sell out for all the wrong reasons." He nuzzled her neck with his lips. "Although, the thought of people watching you cum and seeing that beautiful rose flush in your cheeks ...that's kind of hot."

"Kinky."

"Guilty. What about you? Have you any kinks I should know about?" He finally pulled out of her and lay on his side, his hand stroking her belly. Ama smiled up at him.

"You know, it's hard to tell, because when I'm with you, there isn't anything I wouldn't try. But I don't think I have enough experience to start thinking that way yet. If you want to suggest some things, I'm willing to consider them."

"Hmm." Enda stroked her cheek with his finger. "Not sure. I'm sure we can come up with something together—no pun intended." He slid his arm around her shoulders and hugged her to him. Ama snuggled into his arms and breathed in the night air wafting in through the open windows.

"This place is heaven."

Enda smiled. "I'm glad you like it. Listen, I was thinking ...not wanting to stand in your way or anything, but have you thought any more about going back to San Francisco?"

Ama felt a wave of nausea. Being so close to Jackson again ...but then, there was her work to consider. "I keep going over it in my mind. I don't want to be driven out of the job I adore because of Jackson and his threats, and I owe the conservatory at least a proper goodbye if I leave. My contract stipulates three months' notice."

"Sounds like you've been considering leaving."

Ama nodded, her eyes serious as she looked up at him. "Truthfully, Enda, I have. I would be happy never to go back to the States. This place feels like home to me. *You* feel like home. I mean ..." She went red and sat up, suddenly shy. "I'm not expecting you to ...I don't want to make you feel like you're stuck with me, is all."

Enda chuckled. "*Piccolo*, I'm in this for the long haul. For good. You have no need to worry about that." He ran his hand down her back. "As soon as the divorce is finalized, I would like to ...well, I don't want to make any demands of you, but I would be honored if you would think about ...a commitment of some kind. Engagement, marriage, whatever we both want. Even just a commitment ring, if you feel like you don't want to be legally tied to someone else. Whatever works for us. I love you, Amalia, and this is it for me. You are my person."

Ama tried not to let the tears in her eyes fall. "You always know how to make me feel like the most loved person in the world. Thank you, baby." She pressed her lips to hers, then pushed him back onto the bed, climbing on top of him. Enda cupped her breasts in his hands, then traced the indented line down her stomach to her navel. She shivered with pleasure as he circled it with his fingertip, her own hands reaching for his still half-erect cock and stroking it until he groaned and she lowered herself onto it, sighing as it filled her cunt.

"God, Enda, I will never get tired of this ...never ..."

THE NEXT DAY, Amalia met Inca for lunch in the town. They found a little trattoria and ordered a light seafood linguini and salad for lunch. Since being in Italy, she and Inca had grown incredibly close, and now Ama couldn't remember when they hadn't been friends. Inca was sweet, funny, very intelligent, and was so full of empathy for others that Ama marveled at her capacity for love.

They also had the same sense of humor—bordering on raunchy—and they often talked about their men in their lives. Inca was obviously still head-over-heels for Raffaelo even after all this time.

"He was a tough cookie to fathom when I met him," she admitted now as they ate, "But just his presence used to send my body reeling with desire. Honestly, he's my walking, talking aphrodisiac."

Ama grinned. "I know how you feel ...except my lightning bolt moment happened when I was walking down the aisle to marry Enda's brother. Talk about awkward."

Inca's cheek flushed scarlet then, and she tried to hide a smile. Ama squinted at her.

"What's this ...gossip? What are you hiding, Sardee-Winter?"

Inca grinned. "Oh, you might as well know. Tommaso was my boyfriend first, before Raff. And then it was Raff. And there was a little ...overlap."

"You cheated on Tommaso."

Inca shook her head. "No."

"He knew?"

"Yes."

"And he didn't mind?"

"No." Inca looked at her steadily.

"So, you were sleeping with both of them ..." Suddenly Ama got it and gave a shocked giggle. "*Both* of them? At the *same time*?"

Inca grinned. "Guilty. Are you shocked?"

Ama processed this new information. "No," she said finally, "Not shocked. Definitely not judging you, either, just F.Y.I. Kind of ...envious? I'd love to be that uninhibited."

Inca looked relieved. "Eventually, it had to come to a choice though ...and Tommaso knew that, although I did love him, it was Raffaelo who had my heart. And then I got stabbed, which kinda put a little of the wrong kind of kink in the relationship for a while," she quipped, grinning, and Ama was amazed at her ability to joke about it.

"The thing with Enda and me ...I was a virgin before him."

"You were?"

Ama nodded. "And although the sex is mind blowing, I'm a little scared to ...suggest anything more adventurous yet."

Inca nodded sympathetically. "Before the Winter twins, believe me, I wasn't nearly as *open*, shall we say. I think it's just the matter of being with that one person who you can entirely trust in."

Ama smiled at her friend gratefully. "Thank you for sharing your experience with me, Inks. It does help ...and, girl, you were *wild*."

Inca laughed. "I'm still wild, just with Raff now, as it was meant to be. I also have a great relationship with Tommaso now. I think because he has changed so much and grown more content in himself. He was unsteady emotionally when I met him. Our time together ...I think it both messed with him and helped him, too, as strange as that may seem. Anyway, now he's with Bo and their quadrillion kids. They're coming over soon ...I can't wait for you to meet them."

AMA WAS STILL THINKING about what Inca had said as she drove back to the villa. She felt a pang. She missed her own friends—Lena, Christina, and her sister. She would try to invite them all to Italy, although they had to be careful. Enda had made sure their tracks were covered, so Jackson couldn't find them. Yes, he probably knew they were in Italy, but where, he wouldn't be sure.

In the three months since she'd left him, they had only communicated once, through their lawyers. Jackson wasn't going to give her a divorce or an annulment. She would have to wait for the two years before she could divorce him. She had even tried to say that he could claim she cheated—because, technically, she did—but he just wouldn't even consider it. She didn't want his money or anything from him, but her freedom.

That they hadn't heard from him since was a relief to her, but she knew it made Enda uneasy.

"He's planning something," he would fret, but she had told him.

"This is what he wants. He wants us to be nervous, to be constantly looking over our shoulders. No. I refuse to live like that. What will be, will be."

SHE WALKED into the villa now. It was silent, but cool—a relief from the hot sun outside. Enda was still at work, still planning on building music schools with Raffaelo, but currently catching up on the work he'd let slide when he was in the States. Ama dumped her bag, changed into shorts and a halter-neck top, and checked the time. Four p.m.

She hadn't wanted any staff when they moved here, and Enda had agreed. So, now only a light security team were on the premises, but they worked the perimeter of the grounds and the house was a private sanctuary for Ama and Enda.

She went to the cool, open-plan living area and sat down at the piano. She thought of the beautiful Bösendorfer that Jackson had bought her, trying to curry favor, and realized she preferred this much older, well-loved instrument here. Enda had told her his mother used to play on it and so it felt more like a friend than an object. Ama ran her hands over the keys and played a few bars of various compositions; Mozart, Bach, Copland. She closed her eyes and let her fingers move of their own accord with a new composition, light but sensual ...a love song. She hadn't written anything for months now, it seemed, but as her fingers moved across the keys, she could feel the imperative within her. She switched to modern music —Tori Amos, Sarah McLachlan, Norah Jones—singing along softly with the music.

"I had no idea your singing voice was so beautiful."

Ama turned and smiled at Enda. "Ha. Thank you. It isn't, but thank you anyway." She started to stand, but he waved her down and joined.

"Stay, and play some more for me."

So, she did. With Enda's arms locked around her waist, she played through some of her own compositions for him. Neither of them noticed it had gotten dark by the time she had finished. Enda pressed his mouth to hers.

"That was glorious. *Grazie, cara mia.*"

Ama leaned into his embrace. "You, music, and this beautiful place. I'm in heaven."

She felt his arms tighten around her. "I'm glad you feel that way, *piccolo.*"

Ama stayed in his embrace for a moment, then her stomach growled and they both laughed. "I hadn't realized it was so late. I was going to make us some supper."

"Let's cook together."

. . .

THEY WENT into the kitchen that Ama had grown to love. Exposed brickwork and old-fashioned fixtures belied the state-of-art kitchen equipment. She opened the vast fridge. "It's too hot for curry," she said, grinning at his disappointment. Since meeting her, Enda had become addicted to spicy meals. "Well, I suppose I could do a light vegetable one, and we could have it with salad and roti?"

Enda grinned. "Sounds good to me ...but you may be right about the heat. Maybe something lighter for tonight?"

Ama laughed. "Look at us all domesticated." She turned back to the fridge and made a decision. "Stir-fry?"

Enda nodded. "Sounds good."

THEY ATE out on the terrace, over-looking the Bay of Naples, Enda's hand on her thigh. Ama was thinking about what Inca had said earlier. "Isn't it weird that, when you meet the right person, anything goes?" she said now to Enda.

"I know what you mean. I keep thinking back to that day. Your wedding day. You might think I'm the kind of guy who does that all the time, but no. It was just a confluence of events and feelings, and I thought what the hell? You looked so sad, *Piccolo*. It got me here." He touched his chest. "I felt as if I couldn't breathe until I kissed you."

Ama was moved. "Ditto." She grinned mischievously. "I was talking to Inca today ...she was pretty wild when she was younger. Not that she's old now, but you know what I mean."

Enda grinned widely. "I do."

Ama studied him. "You know? About?"

"The three of them? Yup. It was quite the scandal here back then. Well, not really scandal ... not like it would have been back in the States."

She stroked his hair. "I think I would be too jealous to share you."

Enda kissed her. "Yeah, that scene isn't for me."

"What is? You know, I would try anything with you. Anything."

Enda wiped his mouth on his napkin and studied her, a grin on his handsome face. "Okay ...challenge extended. Let me fuck you somewhere we could get caught."

Ama chuckled, a thrill going through her. "For example?"

"We have that benefit in town later this week. We could sneak behind a pillar and go for it."

Ama considered, then stuck out her hand. "Challenge accepted."

Enda laughed. "There's a part of me that hopes we do get caught."

"You know what," Ama said, smiling widely. "Me too."

JACKSON GALLO PICKED up the phone. "Tell me you've found my wife."

His detective, Larry, chuckled. "And then some. They're in Sorrento, as you thought. They have a villa—pretty comprehensively guarded, but both of them go out quite freely. Your wife had lunch with another woman today. Another Indian woman? Her sister?"

"No, her sister is still here in the US. That must be Inca, Raffaelo Winter's wife. They were unprotected?"

"As far as I could see. Want me to kill her?"

"No," Jackson said sharply, "If anyone's going to kill my wife, it's me this time. The Winter woman ...maybe. Another Penelope situation for her, I think. But not yet. I want to have all the pieces in place before I hit them with it all. What I have planned for them ...they won't have dreamed up in a million years. I don't just want to kill my wife. I want to destroy her, my bastard brother, and anyone else who loves them before I finally kill Ama. I can wait for the right moment."

He gave Larry some final instructions just to keep watching and reporting. Putting down the phone, he smiled to himself. What he had planned wasn't just murder.

It was a slaughter.

AMA LAY in Enda's arms as he slept. It was past midnight, but she couldn't get to sleep at all. She wondered what was bothering her and couldn't get a grip on it. Something was changing inside of her, and she couldn't figure out whether it was physical or emotional or *...what the hell is it?* she thought in frustration, but the answer would not come. She gazed at Enda's sleeping face. In rest, he looked so much younger, less stressed, more boyish. *I love you, so much*, she thought as she looked at him. *I can't imagine my life without you.*

The thought of being without him made her feel sick, and she gently extracted herself from his grip and went into the bathroom. The nausea passed, and she brushed her teeth again, looking in the mirror. Something was different with her. Her face looked fuller, her eyes sparkled, and her hair hung long and lustrous down her back. Her breasts seemed larger and her belly softly curved. Was it just that, finally, she saw herself as a sexual being? More confident? *Maybe*, Ama thought now.

"Hey, you okay?" Enda had woken and was standing naked in the doorway, eyes sleepy, his dark curls wild about his head. He looked adorable.

Ama grinned and went to him, pressing her nakedness against him and feeling his cock respond. She brushed her lips against his. "Fuck me, Enda ...fuck me *hard* ..."

A thrill of danger and arousal flooded her as he pushed her roughly against the wall, his mouth harsh against hers. He spread her legs with his foot. "Open them wide for me, woman."

She did, grinning, and his cock, huge and swollen, thrust hard into her. His fingers bit into her skin as his teeth did the same to her shoulder. She gasped at the pain, but clawed his back with her finger-nails, urging him deeper into her. He tumbled her to the floor and pressed her knees to her chest, driving himself into her as hard as he could, almost violent in his actions. Ama screamed her pleasure to him, calling out his name over and over, urging him to be rougher. He slammed her hands to the cool tile with his, growling his need for her, his cock plowing deeper and faster with every stroke until she came explosively, her whole body shaking violently. Enda pulled out and came on her skin, creamy cum spattering over her belly and breasts. His thumb delved deep into her navel, finger fucking her as he bit down on her nipples, then crushed his lips against hers until she tasted blood.

It was feral, animal, and they tore at each other as they fucked. Enda thrust into her perfect ass, hooking her legs over his shoulder. "God, you're so goddamn beautiful, Ama, I could spend my life just fucking you over and over and over again ..."

Ama came quickly, quivering and shuddering. "Enda ...please ... nail me to the floor. Fuck me everywhere ..."

And they did. They spent all night fucking each other in every room in the villa, even the tiny utility room. Ama sat on the washer as Enda thrust into her again and again.

By the time dawn came, they were sated and exhausted. This time, Ama had no trouble falling asleep.

THE SAME NIGHT, Raffaelo Winter was also having trouble sleeping. For some reason, although he and Inca had made love as usual—rapturous love—when she had fallen asleep, something was nagging at him too.

He got out of bed and went to get some water, staring out of the window over the Bay. Lights of the boats in the Bay bobbed around, and the night was serene.

But he felt something. Something was coming. Lurking in the shadows, waiting. Watching. He emptied the glass and went back to the bedroom. For a long moment, he stood at the door, watching his wife sleep. Her long, dark hair clouded around her on the pillow, her thick, dark lashes resting on her downy cheeks. Her beauty had always made him weak. The last ten years with her had made him happy beyond what he thought was possible.

And yet ...

He was always that someone would try and take her away from him. Inca had survived so many attempts on her life—both offenders were thankfully dead now—but he was always tensed for the next attack. Her beauty attracted admirers and obsessives.

His mind flipped to his friends now. Enda and Ama had fitted seamlessly into their lives here, but the woman his friend had fallen in love with had a little too much in common with Inca for Raffaelo's liking. Jackson Gallo was very much alive and well and was undoubtedly planning his revenge. And who knew who would be caught in the crossfire?

Yes, Raffaelo thought grimly. Something is coming.

And I know, I just know ...nothing good can come of it ...

Selima Rai picked her phone up and saw it was her sister calling. She glanced quickly at the sleeping man beside her and scooted gently out of bed. She went into the living room, slipping into Chase's t-shirt before she answered the call. "Hey, sis."

"Hey, I didn't wake you, did I?"

"Not at all."

"Why are you whispering?" Ama sounded amused and Selima chuckled.

"Hot guy asleep in next room."

"Good work." Ama laughed. "Sorry to call so early. I always forget the time difference."

"I don't care. It's lovely to hear your voice. How are you?"

"Beyond good. How's your program going?"

Selima was studying for her Master's degree in criminology and was loving every day, even though it was hard work. "Good, darling, really. I like my tutors a lot; they're more like friends at this point."

"Suck up."

Selima laughed. "You know it. God, Ama, I miss you."

"Oh, me too, boo. So much. When your semester is over, promise me you'll come to Italy?"

Selima smiled into the phone. "Try and stop me."

Ama seemed to hesitate then. "How is your protection working out?"

Selima's smile faded. "So far, so good. They're very discreet, but still ...I could do without them. I have Chase now."

"Chase, is it? Well, he's probably not going to be locked and loaded, is he, so the protection stays. Sorry, sis." Ama chuckled. "But tell me more about Chase."

LATER, when Chase got up and sleepily lurched into her bathroom to shower, Selima took stock of what her sister had said. Selima was overjoyed that Ama had split from Jackson Gallo. The man was a creep who had kept hitting on her throughout his engagement to Ama. But the repercussions of how they had split up had crashed through Selima's life here in Los Angeles. Jackson Gallo's threats to her own safety had shocked Selima, but his obvious rage and obsession with her sister scared her more. She had no doubt at all that Jackson would harm Amalia if he could, and although Selima was glad Ama was with Enda, she didn't know Enda at all well and didn't know if she could trust him to protect her sister. It made her sick to the stomach to think of Ama being hurt.

Chase came into the kitchen, stealing a piece of toast from her plate. She had met him only recently. He was a new transfer in from a college in Minnesota, and he had a warm, guileless charm that she loved. He'd grinned at her across a lecture hall, and although she tried to play it cool, her stomach filled with butterflies. Turned out, he was a friend of one of her friends and on a group night out, they had gotten to talking. Since then, he'd stayed every night.

He bent to kiss her now, tasting of toast and toothpaste. She wrinkled her nose. "Yuck."

Chase laughed a deep rumble through his broad chest. He was absurdly tall—nearly six-seven—with blonde hair sticking up in every direction, big blue eyes, and an easy smile. "That's what a man likes to hear when he kisses his woman."

Selima grinned. "Who said I'm your woman?"

"Me. And I don't mean that in a caveman, ugg ugg, beat you over the head and drag you to my cave way. I mean, you're my favorite woman, is all."

"That's nice. Thank you. And so was the kiss."

"Oh, I know." He was cocky, self-assured, and safe in his masculinity. Selima loved that about him. Here was a man not threatened by a strong woman. "Now," he said, coming over to her and lifting her onto the table. "I need to have a good breakfast." He pulled her silky robe open and looked around. "Ah ha." He grabbed the little jug of maple syrup and Selima giggled as he poured it over her breasts, then bent to lick it off. "Lay back for me, darlin'."

She did, and he smiled down at her, drizzling the syrup onto her belly so it filled her navel, then down into her sex. He dropped to his knees and ran his tongue from her navel down to her cunt, pressing her legs apart so he could taste her properly. His tongue lashed around her clit and Selima gave a little moan of pleasure. "Just relax there, baby. Let Chase take care of things."

His mouth on her, sent her senses reeling, and when he stood and freed his cock from his jeans, she almost wept at the feel of it plunging into her red, swollen cunt. "God, yes, Chase, harder ..."

Grinning, he fucked her expertly, leaving her gasping, panting for air, and arching her back from the table as she came. Chase groaned, pumping cum deep inside her, then gathered her into his arms to kiss her. "God, baby, where have you been all my life?"

Selima kissed him back. "Just tell me we can do that every day."

Chase grinned. "Sure thing ...although we're gonna go through a *lot* of maple syrup."

SHE WAS STILL GLOWING as she made her way to class later that day, and didn't see the man watching her.

ENDA AND RAFFAELO arrived at the restaurant just before their client and were sitting, chatting, when he arrived. Roger Fallwell was an American property broker who dealt with all the major property scions around the world, but Enda and Raff were surprised when he called them to talk about their project. He had wanted to meet with them on this specific day, at one p.m. and was very adamant about it, which make them scratch their heads.

"Maybe he's just here for one day? How did he even find out about it?" Enda wondered now, and Raff shook his head. "No idea."

Enda shrugged. "Ah, well."

Raff grinned. "You are so chilled out these days, my brother."

Enda chuckled. "Ama," was all he said, and Raff smiled. "Gotcha."

Enda grinned to himself. Last night had been the benefit they had talked about, and he had indeed fucked Ama in a dark alcove, where anyone could have walked past and caught them. No one did, though, but it had been a thrilling ride anyway.

AT HOME, Ama was practicing a piece she had written over and over when her phone rang. "Ama?"

It was Christina, her best friend. Ama was delighted, but Christina's voice was trembling. "Chrissy, what is it?"

"I'm not sure ...someone broke into my home this morning. I was at the store buying milk. They left a message."

Ama's heart began to beat faster. "Chrissy, are you okay? Are you hurt?"

"No ...no, I'm not hurt. I don't think this is about me. Ama, the message was written in blood on my wall. It said ...'Tell her *everyone*, until she's the only one left.' Sweetheart, I think ..."

"...it's Jackson. Chrissy, I want you to pack a bag and get out of there *now*. Did you call the police?"

"I did; there's an officer here. I told them what I told you and they agree – I need to leave for the time being. Darling ...there's something else. There was a fire at the conservatory. No one was hurt, but there was a lot of damage."

Ama's legs gave out, and she slumped to the floor, panting for air. Her chest felt as if it were in a vise. "Chrissy ...my sister ..."

"I already thought about that. There are police on the way to her apartment right now."

"Thank you. Thank you. Chrissy, get out of there now."

"I will, I promise. Keep in touch, Ama, please. Be safe."

"You too. I love you."

ENDA CHECKED his phone and saw three missed calls. *Damnit.* He'd forgotten to switch it off silent mode. He saw the calls were from Ama and he frowned. Just then, though, their guest arrived.

Roger Fallwell looked sweaty and pale as they shook hands, and Enda realized he was trembling. Was he going to have a heart attack? "Are you okay, Mr. Fallwell?"

Fallwell closed his eyes, muttering something to himself. "I can't do this. I can't do this ..."

Enda and Raffaelo exchanged worried glances. Raff cleared his throat and signaled to the waiter. "Could we have some ice water, please? Our guest is unwell."

Fallwell shook his head. "No, it's okay, I'm not ...god, oh god ..."

As they looked on in amazement, Roger Fallwell started to sob.

INCA WAS at her favorite tea house in the city, the one she had opened with Raff soon after they became engaged. With an upstairs tea room over-looking the Bay, it was always busy, and Inca liked to help out as much as she could. It made her feel less like the princess in the ivory tower. The staff and customers alike adored her, and she loved spending time there. It had also improved her Italian exponentially, and she could chatter away to people easily now. She often told Raff that she felt more Italian than American now and she knew he was pleased.

Today, the upper tea room was packed, but downstairs was quiet and cool. Inca took the opportunity to go down and clean. She didn't see the two men enter behind her until one of them cleared their throat. They were dressed casually and wore friendly smiles, and she grinned back. "Hey, fellas, come on in. We have plenty of room. Upstairs or down. I'm Inca, so if you need anything, just ask."

The two men looked at each other and for a second Inca wondered if they had understood her.

Then the large man grabbed her so quickly she couldn't react, clamping a huge hand over her mouth and easily holding her arms with the other massive arm. Without hesitation, the other man stepped forward.

Terrified, Inca only saw a brief flash of steel before he drove the knife into her belly again and again.

The pain was unimaginable.

ENDA TRIED to calm their guest down. "Sir, please ...what is it?"

Fallwell gasped and gulped and finally calmed himself. "He has my wife and my four-year-old daughter. He told me he'll kill them unless I brought you here today, at this time. Both of you."

Both Enda and Raff knew instantly. *Jackson.* Raff leaned forward. "What does he want, Roger? Why bring us here today?"

Roger looked at Raff with sorrow-filled eyes. "I'm so sorry, Mr. Winter ...he wanted her unprotected."

Raff's color drained from his face. "No ...*no* ...not Inca ..."

Roger started to sob again, nodding. "And, Mr. Gallo, he told me to tell you ...this is it. This is where they all die, including Amalia."

STELLA, the tea house's barista heard the scream from downstairs and hurried down. At first, she just saw the shocked tourist standing at the doorway, her hands at her mouth, staring down at the ground. As Stella rounded the corner, her heart almost failed.

Inca was splayed on the floor, eyes closed, with blood spreading everywhere across her dress. Dark purple knife wounds were on her stomach and belly. Her breathing was ragged and hitching, and as Stella dropped to her knees, Inca opened her eyes. In them, she saw confusion, bewilderment, and agony. On the floor beside her was a lethal-looking knife, covered in blood. The tourist was crying, but was on her phone, obviously calling the emergency services.

"*Oh, mio Dio, mio Dio.*" Panicked, Stella pressed her finger gently to Inca's throat. There was a weak pulse, but it was slowing.

Inca made a strange noise, like she was fighting for breath, and then her eyes closed and her head slumped to the side. Stella knew instantly.

Inca was dying.

Then Stella too started to scream for help.

RAFF WAS out of the restaurant in a second, his face yellow with terror, his phone to his ear. Enda followed him, trying to call Ama, but the phone was engaged. As he reached Raff, the other man was talking to someone on the phone. He looked at Enda, and there was untold grief in his green eyes.

"Oh god, no, please ...yes, yes. No, I'm coming now ...god, please, Stella ...tell me she's still breathing ...thank god ...I'm on my way."

He turned to Enda, who was still trying to call Ama. "Inca was stabbed. It's bad, Enda. It's so bad ...god ... I have to go. Get to Ama, *now*. This is Jackson. I know it."

ENDA DROVE like a madman back to the villa, still unable to reach Ama on the phone. As the car screeched to a halt outside, he could see his security team in disarray, and it was only when Ama flew out of the house and into his arms, obviously healthy and apparently safe, that he could breathe again.

But Ama was hysterical, and he couldn't understand what she was saying at first.

"Baby, calm down. Tell me. Calm down ..."

"He has her, Enda ...he has my *sister* ..."

Oh god ...*Selima* ...Enda was staggered at the scope of Jackson's revenge plan. First Inca, now Selima.

"What does he want?"

Ama looked like she was about to pass out. "Me. He told me he will kill her unless I go to him."

"No ...no ...not going to happen."

"Enda, I don't have a choice. Do you honestly think he won't go through with it if I don't?"

Enda closed his eyes and thought about Inca. *No ...Jackson would happily kill Selima.*

Just like he would, without a doubt, murder Ama the moment she went to him.

THERE WERE no happy endings here ...

AMA SAT on the cold tile of the bathroom floor, her head in her hands. Thankfully, the nausea that had attacked her so suddenly in the night had passed. Enda tilted her head up gently and pressed a cold flannel to her burning forehead. Her eyes were puffy from lack of sleep and crying, but Enda was concerned about the utter despair in them.

Jackson had taken Selima and had ordered a hit on Inca, who was fighting for her life in a local hospital after two of Jackson's men had brutally stabbed her and left her for dead.

Raff's voice on the phone had sounded like it coming from the grave. "They're still operating ...they said she'd been stabbed nine times ...*oh god* ...I thought that part of our lives was over. I don't know if she'll make it, Enda. I really don't." He sounded broken.

She's going to die ... Enda pushed the thought away. *Come on, Inks ... you can survive this ...you must.*

When he'd told Ama about Inca, just after she'd had the news that Selima was abducted, she'd collapsed, screaming and sobbing great, wrenching sobs. Enda knew she blamed herself, but now he was more concerned by her silence than her screams.

The police had told them to sit tight while they contacted Olivier, and an hour later, Olivier had called them.

"He's obviously been planning this for months," Olivier said, sounding as desolate as they did. "He emptied his accounts and sold most of the stuff from the house. When they went there tonight, it was on fire. It was gutted ...the house is gone, man. All dad's stuff. Enda, he's got unlimited funds. He can hide anywhere in the world and he won't stop until Ama's in his grip."

"Not going to happen," Enda said grimly. "He'll kill her the minute she goes to him."

"Agreed. Look, my suggestion is to stay there. It's too dangerous here, even though I don't think Jackson is even in the States anymore. He's gone underground. Someone, somewhere surely will have to see him sometime, right? I've already sent out a team to scour California."

Enda sighed. "Good. I'll do the same here. Listen, Tommaso Winter said the same thing. We need to cover the globe. He spoke to Raffaelo—you can imagine what he said."

"How is Inca?" Olivier's voice was soft; he loved Inca as much as the rest of them.

"Not good, brother. Not good at all. God, poor Raff."

"What is this, now? The fourth or fifth attempt on her life? That's way too much for any lifetime."

Enda tried not to let the tears in his eyes fall. He pinched them shut with his fingers. "Let's hope we can still say it was only an *attempt* when this is all over. Raff won't survive if Inca dies."

There was a heavy silence on the other end of the phone. "Enda ...when we find Jackson," Olivier hesitated, then sighed. "You know what I'm going to say."

"Yes," said Enda in a hard voice. "And to answer you ...yes. I want that fucker dead. I know he's your brother, but ..."

"He's no brother of mine," Olivier said. "Live or die ...he's dead to me now."

Enda heard the heartbreak in Olivier's voice and felt the weight of responsibility. His older brother had always been the peacemaker— the steadying hand. Enda hated that he was alone in San Francisco, dealing with all this. "Come to Italy," he urged. "Be with us."

Oliver gave a short, sad laugh. "Believe me, I'd like nothing better ...but someone needs to be here. Besides, Selima's boyfriend could still give us some information."

Chase, Selima's boyfriend of a few weeks, had been shot and critically wounded when Selima was abducted. He had been trying to defend his girlfriend and took a bullet to the chest.

"Fuck," said Enda, "What a mess."

Olivier sighed. "Yeah ...and right now, I just don't see how it could get any worse."

A WEEK later and nothing had changed. Ama stared out of the window at the heavy security around their villa and felt like a prisoner. Not just here in Italy—but of Jackson's. He hadn't contacted her again after that first call, when he'd sounded so triumphant.

"I told you there would be no limit to what I could do if you defied me, Amalia ...now say hello to your little sister."

Selima's sobs—her cries of pain—as Jackson obviously inflicted harm on her, wherever he was holding her. Ama had screamed at Jackson, but he'd merely laughed and told her to wait for his next call.

A week. Doing God knows what to Selima ...*fuck.*

She went to look for Enda, who was in his office with Tommaso Winter and their respective chiefs of security.

She nodded at Tommaso. He looked desolate. Inca was in a coma, still hovering on the brink of life, and Ama knew Tommaso was trying to keep it together and support his brother as Inca fought to recover. Tommaso smiled at her, his eyes tired and heavy. Ama touched Enda's arm.

"Baby, can I talk to you for a minute?"

Enda nodded and followed her out of the room. She led him into their bedroom and closed the door. Enda opened his arms, and she went into them. He kissed her tenderly. "Are you okay, *Piccolo?*"

She shook her head. "No. I just needed alone time with you. I can't bear all this worry and sadness. I think I'm going mad."

Enda sighed and hugged her tightly to him. "I know."

Ama tilted her head up to kiss him again. "Let's just make the world go away for a few minutes."

"You sure?"

She nodded and his fingers pulled at the belt of her wrap dress. Pushing back the fabric and letting the dress fall to the floor, he kept his hands gentle on her skin as he lay her down on the bed. He pulled her panties down and found her wet for him already. "Don't wait," she whispered.

Enda stripped quickly and lay on top of her. "No matter what ...I love you," he said softly, and she nodded, tears in her eyes, as his cock pushed into her.

They made love slowly, rocking gently as his thrusts grew more intense. They gazed at each other, as if drinking each other in, and both their orgasms were mellow, shivering things. When she came, all her suppressed emotion flooded to the surface and Ama began to cry hot, silent tears.

She cried herself out in Enda's arms, and finally, thankfully, fell asleep.

RAFFAELO STROKED the hair away from his wife's face. "Her color is a little better."

Bo Kennedy, his brother's partner, couldn't see any improvement. It made her sick to see Inca so still and pale. Her usually glowing honey skin was yellow and gray, tubes stuck in her arms, and the breathing apparatus filled her throat. *Jesus ...how the hell had this happened? Why? Some sick psycho's way of getting revenge on his wife was to kill her friend?*

Bo sat down heavily in the chair opposite Raffaelo and took Inca's cold hand. She couldn't die ...could she? Not after everything she'd gone through to get to the happy life she had with Raffaelo.

"Whoever this Jackson Gallo wanker is, I'd like to kill him. What a fucking coward. Send two men to kill a defenseless woman? For what? Spite. *Fucker.*"

Raffaelo, his green eyes heavy and exhausted, nodded. "I know ... that's what gets me ...the sheer spite of it. Inca had nothing to do with Ama's decision to leave Jackson." He smiled briefly. "Although, Inca did knee him in the balls."

Bo half-smiled. "Still ...deciding to have her killed for that?"

"Sadly, Jackson is that vengeful and that psychotic. He only went after the women. Idiot thinks they're the weaker sex."

Bo was incensed. "Yeah? Then come at me, bro, I'll show you different."

Inca gave a low moan and they both sat up. Raff leaned over his wife as Bo pressed the button for the nurse. "Inca? *Cara mia*? I'm here. Please, open your eyes. Wake up, baby. I love you, please ..."

He was rambling, and Bo was saddened by the desperation in his voice. The nurse came in and looked at them questioningly. Bo suddenly felt stupid.

"She moaned ...we, um, we thought maybe she was waking up."

The nurse smiled at her sympathetically. "Let's hope. Excuse me, sir. I just want to check Mrs. Winter."

Raff moved, looking discombobulated. "Of course, sorry."

She patted his arm warmly. "Let's just hope," she said again. She took a small flashlight from her pocket and checked Inca's eyes, then checked the machines keeping her alive, and her blood pressure. "Okay, well, I'll just get the doctor and we can make a determination."

RAFFAELO AND BO waited impatiently for the doctor to complete his examination. Raff stared at Inca's hand. He was sure her fingers had briefly squeezed his as he held them, but he was so dog-tired and grief-stricken that he told himself he might have been hallucinating.

The doctor stepped back and smiled at them both. "Mrs. Winter does appear to be coming out of her coma."

The relief hit Raff like a sledgehammer and he gave a low gasp of release. Bo went to him and held him up. The doctor patted his shoulder.

"Now, listen, this is very good news—*very* good news, but, Mr.

Winter, your wife has a long way to go. A long way. Her injuries ... remember, we had to remove her kidney and her liver was lacerated. There's still a high risk of infection. The hysterectomy will have taken a toll too. So, long haul. But this is a great positive step forward." He smiled kindly at Raff, who couldn't stop the tears from flooding down his cheeks. "Now, the thing to remember is that it could take days or even weeks, for Inca to emerge fully from the coma. So, be patient. I'll come back later and run some more tests."

Bo hugged Raff to her. "This is good news, bro. Good, good news."

Raff nodded, not trusting himself to speak. He smiled at her and extracted himself to go and sit by Inca.

"I'll go call Tommaso," Bo said softly, "Tell them all the good news."

Raffaelo nodded, his entire focus on Inca now. When they were alone, he leaned over and kissed the side of her mouth, next to the breathing tube. "*Amore mia,*" he said, his voice breaking. "Please come back to me. I don't know how to live in a world without you. Fight, Inca, my beautiful Inca. You've done this before. Fight. Fight to come back to me."

He picked up her hand and brought it to his mouth. God, when she awoke ...he would have to tell her that she had been targeted yet again by a psychopath and that there had been no good reason, other than malevolence, behind her stabbing. That they'd had to fight to save her life for hours in the operating theater.

That the baby she hadn't known they could have, and that she had been carrying for a month, had been murdered in her womb. Their child. Their only child. They'd told them years ago that she wouldn't be able to carry a baby to full-term, even if she could conceive it, to begin with. And that now, they would never get the chance to try again. The killer's knife had sliced through her womb and they had to remove it. Inca would never be pregnant again.

Mio Dio ...Raff closed his eyes and fought against the scream in his throat. *Never again.* He didn't care if he had to keep her in a fortress. No one would ever touch her again—never hurt her again.

And he, Raffaelo, would never fail her again.

. . .

AMA WOKE in the late evening, as she heard raised voices somewhere in the villa. She pulled a t-shirt and a pair of jeans on and went to find out what was going on. She pushed her way into the kitchen and saw Enda arguing furiously with someone. When she shifted position, she saw him and gasped.

Her father had come to Italy. He saw her and rounded on her, his face a mask of rage. "You. This is your fault. My daughter is abducted and I find out about it on the news? This is your doing, Amalia, and ..."

He never finished the sentence, as an incensed and raging Enda punched him out.

HER UNCLE, her beloved Omar, who had come with Gajendra to Italy, put his arm around her shoulders and kissed her temple. "Your father will calm down, Amalia. Give him time."

Exhausted, Ama leaned against him. "I don't want him here, Omar, but I can't tell you how happy I am to see you. I just wish ... god, Omar. She's been gone a week. Who knows what horrors he's putting her through." She lowered her voice. "Omar ...I don't want Enda to know this, but if Jackson will swap me for her, I'll do it. I'll do it right now."

Her uncle looked pained. "Sweetheart, let's not even consider that as an option yet. Or at all. We'll get Selima back. I have spoken to Olivier Gallo, and now to your Enda and his friend. Between us, we can cover the globe to find your sister. And we will."

Amalia rubbed her eyes. "Dads right about one thing—this is my fault. All of it. Selima, Christina ...Inca. God." She felt sick.

Omar tightened his arm around her and spoke in a low, fierce voice. "This is not your fault. Your father is lashing out because he feels the guilt keenly. The guilt for using his daughters to save his business, when he could have come to me. His pride put you both in harm's way. He knows that marrying you to Jackson Gallo was the catalyst. He fed Jackson's obsession and sense of entitlement."

Ama heard his words, but could not shake the guilt anyway. "Omar, could you take dad back to the hotel? I need some time with Enda."

Omar kissed her cheek. "Of course, darling. I will be just a phone call away if you need me."

ENDA LOOKED TIRED, but when she joined him in the kitchen, he kissed her and smiled at her. "Inca's coming out of her coma," he told her, and Ama felt her heart lift.

"Really?"

"Tommaso just called. She's still critical, but it's a good step forward."

Ama slumped against him. "Some good news, at last." She felt like crying, but this time for good reasons. Could this be the tide turning?

"Have they found anything out about Selima's whereabouts?"

Enda hesitated, then shook his head. "I'm sorry, baby. Chase is still unconscious, and the California team has had no luck. Look, we have the house to ourselves tonight. Just for one-night ...let's try and relax and spend some time together. I know it will be difficult, but I'm worried that if we—and I mean you, *Piccolo*—keep this level of stress up, we'll make bad decisions. Forget why we did this."

Ama was silent, considering his proposal. Could she relax, knowing what was happening to her sister? Even if it wasn't happening—and she didn't think there was any chance of that—she still had the visions of what Jackson could do to her sister.

But she looked up into the eyes of the man she had sacrificed everything for and knew she would make the same decision over and over again. Enda was right. They needed to reconnect properly, remember that they were in this together, and that there were more people on their side than on Jackson's.

She nodded up at him. "Yes, okay ...for tonight ...me and you."

"Good." He kissed her forehead. "Let's start by getting some proper food into you. You haven't eaten for days."

They cooked a meal together, a hot and spicy curry that they washed down with a cold beer each, then sat watching TV. Ama couldn't help her mind drifting to her sister, and at ten p.m., Enda looked around at her, studied her expression, and sighed. "Miss Rai ...I think I need to distract you more ..." He stood up and pulled her to her feet. He nuzzled his nose to hers before pressing his lips against hers. "The house is empty except for us. We're totally alone ... listen how quiet the night is."

He led her to the window and pushed open the shutters. The stone window sill was wide enough for them both to sit on. "Look at that," Enda said softly. The moon was full over the Bay of Naples, Vesuvius casting a long shadow. The cities of Naples and Sorrento lay beneath them. The lights of the fishing boats bobbed out at sea, the soft glow from the cities' streets. "There is only one thing I consider more beautiful than this view," Enda said in his low, growly accent, "And that is you, *Piccolo*. You are the love of my life and the reason for my being. There is absolutely no way I would give you up for anything. I know what you think—that you hold Selima's life in your hands. You don't. But you hold mine, and I hold yours. There is no you and me. There is only us. And we, together, will fight this and we will win."

Ama had tears in her eyes and they spilled down her cheeks as he finished speaking. She couldn't speak. Couldn't tell this wonderful man just how much she loved him. Instead, she kissed him, her mouth hungry against his. He pulled her onto his lap and began to peel her dress from her shoulders until he could dip his head and take her nipple into his mouth. Ama sighed and closed her eyes, not caring if any of the security guards patrolling their grounds could see them. *This is what matters*, she thought. *Love*. Enda picked her up and carried her to the couch, pushing up her skirt and snagging his fingers in her panties to pull them off. Ama pulled her dress over her head and then helped him strip, running her hands over his broad shoulders, wide, muscled chest, and flat stomach. He covered her body with his, seeking her lips.

"Ama ..." he murmured, in the way that always made her weak, and as she curled her legs around his hips, feeling his erection nudging at her, she opened up to take him in as deep as she could, wanting and needing that connection.

Enda moved in slow, measured strokes, kissing her, murmuring her name over and over, and sending thrills through her entire being. Ama gazed up into his green eyes and wondered how she had ever existed without this man. She could believe him, in moments like this, that everything would be okay—that everything would turn out right.

He was so controlled that her orgasm built and built, and every time she thought she would reach her peak, Enda would hold back, until she was quivering mass of anticipation. When her orgasm hit, it made her mind whirl, her skin vibrate, and all she could see was him, smiling down at her, groaning as he too came, his seed shooting deep into her belly.

"I love you. I love you," she whispered, and he laughed softly.

"And I'm not even halfway done tonight ..."

THEY MADE love until dawn began to spread its fingers across the sky, then fell asleep, wrapped in each other's arms. When they woke, Ama felt stronger than she had in days. Then, in the evening, the news came that Inca was awake.

Inca awoke sometime in the afternoon, and of course, it was in the five minutes that Raff, who had been at her side constantly, went to take a coffee break. Alone, Inca blinked, trying to get the smeary glaze from her eyes, moving her limbs, feeling the stiffness of her body, and the numbness that she recognized as morphine coursing through her system. It was a heavy dose too, she knew of old—from the *last* time she'd been stabbed. How the hell had it happened again? Here, in her beloved Naples, where all she had found was love. Had it been part of a robbery? Somehow, she couldn't see it. It was personal. She remembered the man who had stabbed her so viciously ...he had looked her in the eye as he plunged the knife into her. The expression she would never forget ...enjoyment. He meant to kill *her*. Inca was sure of it. She wasn't a random victim.

Could it have been Edgar Winter, her husband's psychotic father who had tried to kill her twice before, just to make Raffaelo suffer? He was rotting away in prison now for his crimes, but he could have just as easily hired someone to do it. After all this time, though? It had been years that he had been incarcerated.

Inca moved, and then moaned in pain. Agony screeched through her body, but instead of upsetting her, it just made her angry. Who the hell were these people to decide whether she lives or died? Luna, Kevin, Knox, Edgar ...two of them were dead; Kevin was, like Edgar, in jail. And now those two assholes in her beloved tea house ...

The anger made adrenaline shoot through her body, and she struggled to sit up, ignoring the agonizing pain in her abdomen and gripping the breathing tube to rip it out.

Only the appearance of Bo stopped her from doing it. "Hey, hey, hey, hey ...*no, no, no*, baby. Don't do that." Bo dropped the coffee she was holding and dashed to Inca's side, holding her up with one strong arm and gently pushing her hands away from the tube. "Nurse! Somebody help me!"

Two nurses and a doctor came racing in, and between them, they managed to calm Inca down. She gestured furiously at the breathing tube. The doctor injected her with a sedative. "Mrs. Winter, if you calm down, I can do some checks, and if you're breathing on your own, I'll consider removing the tube. But you have to calm down for me ...your abdomen is recovering from serious wounds and the resultant surgery. If you tear an artery, you will bleed out and die. Okay?"

Inca saw Bo wince. The other woman looked back at her and tried to smile. "Welcome back, gorgeous." She kissed the back of Inca's fingers, and Inca felt her tears on her skin. "Sweetie, while they look after you, I'm going to get Raff—he's only getting some coffee. I'll be right back."

Inca nodded, the effects of the sedative kicking in. The doctor and nurses did their tests, but a few moments later, Inca could only see *him* – her Raffaelo. The look of relief and love on his face was overwhelming, and she thought, as she had done once before, that his smile was better than any painkiller they might give her.

AMA WAS nervous about walking into the hospital room and seeing her friend so hurt and brutalized. She had not been to see Inca when she was in a coma. Raff had wanted to limit Inca's visitors because of the risk of infection, and Enda and he had agreed that it would be too hard on Ama.

Ama was convinced Raff blamed her for his wife's stabbing, even though both Enda and Tommaso assured her nothing could be further from the truth. "He's just gone into over-protective mode. Although, at this point, I wouldn't say anything is too overprotective as far as Inca goes." Tommaso had been almost as devastated by Inca's attempted murder as Raff, and Ama remembered that he, Tommaso, had loved Inca first. She had hugged him. "I love her too," she whispered to him, and he nodded, fighting back the tears.

She saw Raff first, and he came to her and wrapped his arms around her. "She's just sleeping. The pain killers make her so tired."

Ama walked in and tried not to give a cry of horror. Inca had lost a lot of weight. There were dark circles under her eyes, and her lovely face, even in sleep, was creased in pain.

Ama wobbled, and both Raff and Enda steadied her. Ama turned to Raff. "Is she going to be okay?"

Raff drew in a deep breath. "We hope so. It'll be a long road to recovery—even longer than last time. We'll get there. Do you want to sit with her for a while? She should wake up soon."

Ama nodded. "How much does she know? I don't want to upset her."

"Everything. She asked to be told everything. It ...god ...she's stronger than even I realized."

Ama touched his face. "Raff, I'm so sorry about the baby."

He half-smiled, but it was a strained thing. "The strange thing is

...we had made our peace with not having kids. This seems like a cruel joke. As if being stabbed nine times by two men twice her size wasn't bad enough." His voice broke and he looked away. Enda gripped his shoulder.

"Come on, Raff. I'm buying you a strong coffee and something to eat. *Cara mia*, do you mind if we leave you two alone for a while?"

Ama shook her head. "I'll be here with Inca. Take as long as you need."

Inca woke less than ten minutes later, and Ama helped her sip from a cup of water. Inca smiled at her. "Hey, you. How are you? Is there any news?"

Ama bugged at her. "Shouldn't I be the one asking if *you're* okay?"

"Well," Inca looked down at the heavy bandaging around her torso. "I'm going to say I'm all set." She grinned, but then her smile faded. "And don't even think you're responsible for this. Raff told me that's what you told Enda and it's a bunch of crap. This is all Jackson Gallo. Asshole."

'Asshole' was such an understatement when it came to describing Jackson that suddenly Ama got the giggles. Inca looked at her in surprise, then started to laugh too. "Oww, oww, don't make me laugh. My stomach muscles are compromised. Oww!" But she dissolved into giggles too.

"I don't know why I'm laughing," Ama said, wiping her eyes, "You're in here, my sister's still missing, and Jackson ..."

"Is still breathing," Inca said, her smile fading. "Girl, if you can wait until I'm mobile, I say you and me go Black Ops on his ass."

"From your lips to God's ear, Inks. But seriously now, I am so sorry you got dragged into this. I can't imagine what it was like."

Inca winced a little as she shifted in the bed. "Personal. That's the word I keep coming back to. The man who stabbed me ...it was personal for him. He enjoyed it. He got off on sticking that knife in my belly. Jackson's surrounded himself with men like him. Psychotic, sociopathic, and devoid of empathy. They like to kill, and they like to kill women."

Ama dropped her head in her hands and moaned. "Inks...I can't sit around waiting for Jackson to kill Selima. I know the men are doing everything their money will allow. It's not enough."

Inca was studying her. "Now I know you're not thinking about going to Jackson?"

Ama met her gaze. "If it was a choice between you and Raffaelo ... what would you do?"

"Jesus, Ama ...you can't ask me that. Goddamn it." Inca's voice broke. "I wish you hadn't told me. Please, darling, I'm begging you. Don't give in to him."

Ama shook her head. "No, you misunderstand me. I have no intention of giving into him. I'm going to kill him."

AMA WAS quiet on the way back to the villa that night, and when they got home, Enda sent the staff home and they went to their bedroom. Enda sat on the bed. "What's going on in that mind?" he asked gently.

Ama sat next to him, brushing her fingers through his hair. "Enda ...I think we need to go back to San Francisco."

Enda looked at her, and she could see the conflict in her mind. Finally, he sighed. "I've been thinking the same thing. We're not getting anywhere here. It's just ...the thought of you being in his sightline."

"We don't know he's there, but I guarantee he'll be watching. We go back. I go back to work as if nothing's changed. We—you and I—will be visible in society. We goad him into contacting me again. We make a deal. Me for Seli—"

"No way. That's not's going to happen, *cara mia*," Enda got up and paced the room. "I agree we should be there, but if you think we're going to use you as bait."

Ama sighed. "I think it's too late to consider anything else, baby. I *am* his bait. I'm what he wants. We've established he could be anywhere in the world, which means I'm already in his sights. He knows we're here. That's why he sent men to kill Inca. He wanted me to know he is always close."

Enda looked unhappy and was silent for a long time, looking out of the window. Finally, he returned to her side. "Fine. But the level of personal security you're getting will be insane, okay? Please. I know you hate the intrusion, but this is your life we're talking about. Until Jackson is ...put out of action ...you'll have to promise me."

Ama nodded slowly and met his gaze. "I promise, Enda. I do. But we're getting Selima back alive."

He pressed his lips to hers and she kissed him back, almost urgently. "Take me to bed, Enda, and fuck me *hard*."

She felt his lips curl up in a smile. "That's my girl."

He pushed her back on the bed and began to unbutton her dress, taking the time to kiss every inch of skin he uncovered. Ama sighed, giving into the sensations he was sending through her. When his mouth found her sex, she shivered, and as his tongue lashed around her clit, she stroked his hair. "Baby, I want to taste you too."

Enda grinned at her, then stepped back, stripped off, and climbed onto the bed so she could take him into her mouth while his tongue returned to tease her clit. His cock filled her mouth, the silky skin of the shaft soft against her exploring tongue, the underlying muscle growing more rigid. She moaned as Enda spread her legs wider and plunged his tongue deep into her cunt. His cock grew hard in her mouth as she teased the sensitive tip with her tongue, and she tasted the salty pre-cum. As they drove each other on, Enda came in her mouth, and she swallowed him down greedily. Almost frenzied in their lust, Enda moved to kiss her mouth, pushing her knees to her chest, and she clawed at his back as he slammed his cock into her, biting down on her shoulders and breasts. She screamed his name as he made her cum over and over, tangling her fingers in his dark curls and pulling hard. It was the most feral, uninhibited fuck they had ever had, and Ama felt strength and ferocity running hot through her veins.

As Enda Gallo, her love and her life, fucked her long and hard into the night, Amalia smiled to herself. *Fuck you, Jackson. You'll never take this away from me.*

You're going down, asshole.

3
___

PART THREE

*S*an Francisco, a week later ...
It was almost as if Ama expected Jackson to be waiting at the airport, Selima in one hand and a gun in the other. The nightmares plagued her. Selima crying, bruised, begging Ama not to do it. Jackson's triumphant grin as he let Selima run to Enda, then shoved the muzzle of the gun against Ama's belly and pulled the trigger.

She shivered. She knew it was ridiculous, but when they landed the private jet at the airport and stepped out into the California sunshine, she scanned the area looking for him. Instead, a dark-windowed town car pulled up, and Olivier—lovely, sweet Olivier got out. Suddenly, she couldn't wait to go down the steps. Olivier swept her up in a bear hug. "God, it's good to see you, little one."

Ama clung onto him. He looked tired and drawn. "I'm sorry we left you alone for so long with this, Olly."

He held her tightly. "As long as you're safe, that's all I care about ... and I bring positive news. Chase is out of his coma and talking. We think Selima is still in the state, but being hidden in an underground facility. After he was shot, Chase said he remained conscious long enough to hear Jackson say to take Selima to the 'facility' and that he "will join them in an hour." The F.B.I. have gone over Jackson's records with a fine-tooth comb. They have a few leads."

Ama's heart was in her throat. "God, really?"

Olivier grinned at her and his brother. "Really. Now let's get you home."

JACKSON GALLO WAS INFORMED that Ama and Enda were back in San Francisco less than half an hour later. He smiled smugly – Ama knew she was in a no-win position and Jackson banked on her doing everything to get her sister back alive.

He moved quickly through the corridors of the underground facility he had purchased after he had become engaged to Ama. He had it fitted out with comfortable rooms, hot water, heating, kitchens, and bathrooms; he knew that Amalia Rai did not want to marry him and he did not want to have to resort to the lengths he had with Penelope. After all, the goal was to sleep with Ama, not kill her—not at first—so if she had defied him, then he would have brought her here and kept her confined until he decided her punishment.

Now it had proved useful for her sister. Selima Rai wasn't as spirited as her sister, but she still tried to attack him every time he went near her. Now she was handcuffed to the bed, and when Jackson went to taunt her, he made sure to stay out of her reach.

He opened the door to her room. Selima glared at him, but didn't get up. Her hair hung in strands around her face. Jackson sighed. "For god's sake, clean yourself up. You look terrible."

"Fuck you, Jackson, I don't have to look pretty for anyone, let alone the man who kidnapped me and killed my boyfriend."

Jackson shrugged. "He got in the way. If you and your sister didn't act like whores, none of this would be happening."

Selima spat at him. "You're pathetic."

Jackson wiped his face. "And, yet, I seem to be holding all of the cards."

"She won't come back to you. I won't permit it. Enda, Olivier ...

they won't permit it. So, you might as well kill me now and cut your losses."

Jackson rolled his eyes. "You know, you could be grateful. There's a cell in this building. A great, hard, cold concrete cell that you could be in. It's only through my good graces that you're keep fed, warmed, and in this luxury." He gestured around the comfortable room with its four-poster bed and big-screen T.V. "Shut your mouth, enjoy what you've got here, and pray I don't kill you the second Ama comes back to me."

Selima went quiet then, and Jackson turned to go. Before he reached the door, she spoke up, her voice breaking.

"Are you going to kill Ama?"

He didn't answer her.

CHASE CAPLAN FELT like a hole had been punched through his chest. *Which, come to think of it, it had,* he thought and grinned to himself. It took a lot to make Chase feel down, but being shot had come pretty close. After waking up from his coma, his first question had been "Is Selima okay?"

When he was told, she was still missing, he hadn't hesitated in asking to talk to the police, and to Olivier. The doctors had wanted him to take it easy. He ignored them.

Today, he would meet Selima's sister for the first time. He wondered how he would feel, seeing someone who resembled his lover so much. In the few weeks, he and Selima had been together, he had fallen hard for the tiny Indian-American woman. Every moment they were together was the most fun he'd ever had, and even though he was a salt-of-the-earth, straight-A, country boy, he found himself acting more spontaneously ...recklessly? Had they been reckless the night Selima had been taken?

There had been a roof party at one of their friend's apartments, and they had stayed late, Selima sitting on his lap as they shared a beach chair. The night had been sultry, lines of twinkle lights strung around the rooftop and soft music playing. Selima had snuggled into his big chest, and he had kissed the top of her head.

"Hey, beauty."

"Hey, you." She'd looked up at him as he kissed her mouth gently. Selima had sighed happily. "God, what a great night."

"Not over yet." He'd grinned at her meaningfully, and she'd laughed.

"You know," she'd lowered her voice. "My place is only about four blocks from here ...but there are a lot of dark alleyways we could take shortcuts through."

He had gotten her meaning and chuckled. "Why, Ms. Rai, you're tryin' to ruin my reputation, huh?"

THEY HAD MADE their way home, ducking into alleyways to make out, and when they had reached the one nearest Selima's apartment, she'd grinned up at him, leaning back against the wall and hitching up her skirt. "Come here, farm boy, and fuck me good."

Chase had laughed, but gathered her to him, pressing her back against the wall and sliding her panties down her legs. Selima's hands had been at his fly, freeing his engorged cock from his underwear. He'd thrust into her, and she'd given a half-shocked laugh at the force of him. They'd fucked silently against the wall, only pausing mid-way as an elderly man walked past the end of the alleyway, stopping to let his dog pee on a dumpster. Selima had started giggling, and Chase had to put his hand over her mouth to silence her.

STUMBLING HOME AFTERWARD, neither of them had seen the men waiting for them. When one had stepped out of the shadows and grabbed Selima, Chase was on him immediately. Then the other guy had begun to pull him away, Selima screaming at them.

"Don't hurt the girl." He'd heard a clipped American accent, glanced around, and recognized Jackson Gall immediately. Jackson had smirked, holding Selima back as the men had whaled on Chase, and when one had knocked him to the ground, the other had pulled out a gun, and Chase had felt his chest explode. Selima had screamed as Chase realized he'd been shot and that he could no longer move his body. His head had whirled as he saw Selima pushed into a car. "Take her to the facility," Jackson Gallo had instructed his men, "I'll follow you in an hour."

Chase had wanted to shout, to scream, to tell Selima he would save her, but he hadn't been able to speak or move. His entire body had been cold—too cold. Gallo had leaned over him and smiled. "I really don't care if you live or die, my friend, but if you live, tell Amalia this ...her sister will suffer the same fate as Penelope and Inca unless she comes back to me. Tell her to wait for my call."

Chase closed his eyes, and for once, let the despair take over him. *Selima, I will do everything I can to find you.* But he felt helpless.

An hour later, he felt the despair even more keenly when Selima's sister walked into the room, took one look at him, and put her arms around him. Then, for only the third time in his twenty-six years on the planet, Chase Caplan cried.

INCA FINISHED ANOTHER BOOK, then put it on the pile next to her bed. Her recovery was going well, but slowly—and she was bored. Raff, Tommaso, and Bo kept her company as much as they could, but Raffaelo was looking for the men who had tried to kill his beloved wife, as well as helping out Enda and Ama, and Bo and Tommaso had seven kids to try to juggle. Stella and a couple of other girls from the tea house had been in to see her, as well as some of her friends from Naples, but they treated her as if she were a fragile thing and Inca had had enough of it. She was pissed, almightily pissed, at being back in this situation.

When Raffaelo came in to see her, she had worked herself up into a temper. "I want out of here, Raff. *Tonight.* I'm not even on any drips or feeds or whatever anymore. I hate this. I hate being here."

· · ·

RAFF LET HER RANT AWAY, holding her hand. The psych doctor had told him to expect this—to expect a kickback from not having processed the attack. Inca had told the police everything, then had not wanted to talk about it again. Neither had she wanted to discuss the baby. Raffaelo could see the heartbreak in her eyes, but she would not even contemplate what their lives would have been like if their child had been born. They had tested the dead embryo and discovered it was a girl, but Raffaelo had not told Inca that. She was particularly close to Tommaso and Bo's only daughter, Hermione (named by their two oldest sons, who were Harry Potter mad), and Raff had caught her looking wistfully at the girl as she played with her brothers.

Damn it. Even his chest cramped up with despair as he thought about how close they had come to being parents. *A little girl,* he thought, *who looked like her beautiful mother and maybe had my eyes.*

But it wasn't to be. Raff waited for Inca to rant herself out, then held her as she started to cry. He knew it was just frustration; Inca wasn't someone who felt sorry for herself.

When she was just hiccupping, and looking embarrassed, he brushed his lips against hers, back and forth, until he felt her lips curve up in a smile. They knew each other so completely now and had perfect trust between them.

Inca drew away and touched his cheek. "Sorry, baby."

"Don't apologize. I love you, *Principessa.*"

She sighed and smiled. "As I love you. Give me some good news, darling."

Raff grinned. "I can, actually. Selima's boyfriend woke up and has given them some great information. They think Jackson has her somewhere in California."

Inca's eyes opened wide. "Wow, that is good news. Are you going to California, then?"

Raff was astonished. "Are you kidding me? I'm not leaving you alone."

"Baby, you have three armed guards outside my hospital room at all times. No one is getting in here."

Raff shook his head. "Inca, there's no doubt in my mind that the men who stabbed you are still in Naples. They will have been told to watch us and possibly finish the job." He swallowed hard and shook his head at that. "Finish the job if you survive. And you *have*. I'm not letting you out of my sight, *Principessa*. I will find them, and I will kill them. I promise you that."

Inca took his hand, seeing his distress. "I love you, Raffaelo Winter."

"*Ti amo*, Inca. *Ti amo*."

AMA AND CHASE talked for hours, until she could see the young man was exhausted. He still protested when she told him he needed to rest. "I'll come back tomorrow, if I may. Enda won't let me go back to work just yet, until he puts all the protection he wants into place, so I'll go crazy stuck at Olivier's house alone."

Chase nodded. "Please do. I'd like you to meet my family when they come visit me."

Ama gingerly hugged him. "Selima has good taste in men."

Chase laughed. "She'll tell you what a doofus I am when she comes home."

They smiled, but the hopelessness they both felt was palpable. Ama shook herself. "We'll get her back, Chase, I promise."

The young man's eyes were serious. "Don't promise that."

Ama nodded. "I'm sorry. I know I shouldn't ...but I will stop at nothing to get her home safely. Goodnight, Chase."

"Night, Ama. See you tomorrow."

HER PROTECTION DETAIL—TWO HUGE, heavily armed men called Trevor and Dustin—drove her back to Olivier's house. When she got home, only Enda was waiting for her. "Olivier's had to go to New York for business overnight."

Ama went into his arms. "God, I missed you today."

Enda smiled and brushed his lips against hers. "And I missed you.

Tell me what Chase said." He led her to the sofa and Ama filled him in on everything Chase had told her. When she repeated Jackson's threat about Penelope and Inca, Enda nodded slowly. "Interesting. So, does he think Inca is dead?"

"I don't know. Raff kept the stabbing out of the papers for Inca's protection. That's all I know."

"Hmm. I talked to Raff earlier. He's convinced the men who attacked Inca are still in Naples. It wouldn't be hard for them to find out she was alive ...so how come they haven't told Jackson that she survived?"

Ama considered this. "Maybe they don't want him to be angry for their failing? Maybe he paid them in full to kill Inca, and because she survived, then maybe it means he'll demand his money back?" She sighed heavily. "Maybe it's because they want to finish the job."

Enda nodded slowly. "Or maybe there's a chink in the armor. Maybe after they stabbed Inca, they had a change of heart."

Ama looked skeptical. "Doesn't seem likely."

"Unless Jackson got cheap and hired non-professionals. After all, a professional hitman would have—and I'm sorry to put this image in your head—made sure Inca was dead. He would have probably shot her in the head and left. These assholes enjoyed the close nature of the attack—stabbing her and watching her suffer. I'd say they were local criminals, and I'd also say ... if we find them, we could get information out of them."

"If Raff doesn't kill them first."

"If that, yes. I'll talk to him."

Ama smiled at her lover. "What would you do?"

Enda's face was set. "They'd be dead the minute I found them. But that won't help anyone."

Ama stroked his face. "Enough now. I'm assuming, because you would have told me already, that there's no news on Selima."

"Right."

Ama sighed. "Then, Enda Gallo, let's go to bed. I need a distraction. I need to release this tension. My whole-body aches because of it, and I can see yours does too. Take me to bed."

. . .

ENDA'S HANDS slid under her dress and he pulled it over her head. His lips were against hers, then trailing down her neck to her full breasts. As he took her nipple into his mouth, his hands were pushing her panties down. Ama stepped out of them and shivered as he teased her nipple until it was hard. Doing the same to the other, his lips then moved down her stomach to her belly, his tongue rimming her navel.

"Enda ..." Her voice was soft, and he stood as she unbuttoned his shirt and his pants. Her lips were soft and sweet on his and Enda felt a rush of adrenaline course through him. Both naked, they tumbled onto the bed, and Ama moved down his body until she could take his cock into her mouth. Tracing the tip of her tongue up the shaft, she teased his sensitive tip until she could taste the salty pre-cum. His cock was rock-hard and trembling under her touch, but before he could cum, he pulled her on top of him and impaled her, his long, thick shaft plunging deep into her velvety cunt. Ama gave a long moan of pleasure, and Enda had to hold back. His hand stroked her clit as she rode him, and he was transfixed by the sight of his cock sliding in and out of her.

"God, you're beautiful, *cara mia.*" The low light in the room made her skin look golden. Her breasts were ripe and plump and her silky belly had that slight curve to it. Her dark hair tumbled in waves over her shoulders and her lovely face was flushed pink from her arousal. Ama began to move quicker as they became more aroused, and Enda's cock swelled and became almost unbearably sensitive.

He came hard, his body jerking and bucking her under as he ejaculated deep inside her. Ama gave a cry of release and shuddered, her breath coming in short gasps as her orgasm rippled through her.

As they caught their breath, Enda pressed his lips to her forehead and Ama snuggled in close to him. They had no need for words.

TWO DAYS LATER, a nervous and trembling Ama returned to the Music Conservatory. As Trevor and Dustin drove her into the city, she realized she was more nervous about facing her colleagues and students than she was about any threat Jackson might be. She was glad that her best friend, Christina, would be there to support her today. Since her apartment had been broken into, Christina had been staying with her boyfriend and had reported no more threats or strange occurrences. When Ama thought about what had happened to Inca, she couldn't help, but be utterly relieved that Jackson had left Christina alone. *Enough people have been hurt,* she thought now as the car pulled up to the school. Maybe today would be the day Jackson would realize she was back and get in touch. She knew it was a long shot that anything would happen the first day back. Jackson wouldn't be so reckless. He would know the security measures Enda had put in place.

But Ama had no doubt that he would be watching. She pushed the thought away. *Act normally, as if he wasn't holding her beloved sister hostage. That will enrage him. Jackson wants the attention.* All the things Enda told her went through her head again now.

Christina met her at the door and the two women hugged for a long moment. "Hey, girl." Christina, her black hair pulled up into a chignon and her slender figure in jeans and t-shirt, smiled at her, but her eyes were worried. "Are you okay?"

Suddenly Ama felt like crying. She nodded, not trusting herself to speak, and Christina smiled, understanding. "Come on. Let's get some of that atrocious coffee they serve in the cafeteria."

A HALF HOUR LATER, she went up to her office. Christina had shown her around the two music rooms that were fire-damaged. "We were lucky someone spotted it before it spread too far, but it's awkward these two being out of use for the time being."

Enda had offered the school the money to repair the damage and would not take no for an answer. Ama felt bad though; it had another 'fuck you' from Jackson toward her.

In her office, Lena hugged her too. "So good to have you back, boss."

Ama smiled. "Sorry to have abandoned you for so long. But I come bearing more news."

Lena studied her. "You're leaving for good, aren't you?"

Ama nodded. "I am. I'm sorry, but I want to be with Enda, and I want to be in Italy. He and Raffaelo Winter are opening music schools across the world, and I'm going to help them." She smiled. "So, if you feel like a change of pace or of country, we could always use superb administrators. But don't tell the dean I said so. I'm already in trouble for giving notice."

Lena nodded, but her eyes were sad. "I'll miss you."

Tears threatened again. "Don't make me cry." Ama smiled at her assistant. "Come on, boss me around for a bit. I'll feel like I'm home then."

Lena grinned. "Okay, well, there's your email folder. Don't even ask how many unread you have. I've tried to sort them into folders in order of importance, and I deleted all the spam, but still. Any marked private, I haven't opened. I promise. They're in a folder on your desktop."

Ama sat down at her desk and flicked her work laptop on. She had left everything behind when she'd fled to Italy, including this old machine, and it took a while for the computer to boot up. She went to put a fresh pot of coffee on and noticed the fine layer of dust covering everything. With a note of sadness, she realized this place was a stranger to her, and she to it.

She had given the dean her notice—three months—and he had been sad, but understanding. Enda had already spoken to him about the extra security, telling him in confidence the situation with Ama and her sister. The Dean had been appalled, of course, and promised to do everything in his power to protect Ama.

Ama sat back down at her desk and clicked open the private email folder. Private messages from an 'unknown' addressee filled the screen. Ama swallowed, knowing they all had to be from Jackson. The first one was dated the night she left him, and it was a rambling, venom-filled email telling her she was a whore and that Enda was a bastard who was only romancing her to pay Jackson back. All vitriolic swill, but nothing Ama wouldn't have expected. She almost deleted it, then paused. It was still evidence, wasn't it? There were a few more angry rants around the same date, but then, for a period of some months, nothing. Then, the day Jackson had abducted Selima, the email started again. Ama clicked on the first one.

Time's up.

With the short phrase was a photograph of the inside of Christina's apartment, trashed, with the bloody messages scrawled across the walls. The second email was a photo of a small fire being set in the music rooms in the conservatory. So, that *had* been Jackson.

Ama didn't want to think about what was included in the few emails left, but she made herself click on them in order.

She gave a squeak of distress. Chase Caplan lying on the sidewalk, blood spread across his t-shirt, his eyes closed. The moment Selima had gone missing.

The next email showed Selima chained to a bed, looking cowed, but thankfully not bruised. Ama studied the photo of her sister minutely, trying to see the expression in Selima's eyes, then trying to place the bedroom. She shook her head, her chest hurting with the pain of knowing her sister was somewhere and she couldn't get to her.

The next email took her breath away. A woman she didn't know lay slumped in the front seat of a car, her dress soaked in blood, the hilt of a knife protruding from her stomach. Dark red stab wounds covered her torso. The woman's soft caramel hair hung to her shoulders, her eyes were closed, and her pretty face still contorted with pain and horror, even in death.

Penelope. *Oh, Jesus Christ, Oh, god, oh god ...* Ama felt nausea rise in her throat.

The last email she hesitated to open. When she did, she saw this one was a video file. From the screenshot at the start, she could see the outside of Inca's teahouse in Naples and knew instantly what she would see. Ama closed her eyes. *I don't know if I can do this ...*

But maybe there would be some clue ...

She hit the play button. Someone, obviously wearing a camera, walked into the cool, shaded lower floor of the tea house. Ama saw Inca cleaning up alone. God, she looked so happy and so beautiful in her little tea-dress. She smiled at the men with the cameras, and Ama heard her say "Hey, fellas, come on in. We have plenty of room. Upstairs or down. I'm Inca, so if you need anything just ask."

Another man, who was with the cameraman, grabbed Inca so quickly it made Ama jump back from the screen. She saw him pull Inca's arms behind her, then saw the confusion and fear in Inca's lovely face. With increasing horror, Ama watched the cameraman pull out the knife and plunged it into Inca's belly. Inca gasped in agony, and Ama gave a moan as she watched her friend being stabbed again and again. When he had finished, the men lay Inca on the floor of the tea house. The whole attack took less than fifteen seconds. The cameraman lingered over Inca's prone body. She was conscious, her eyes confused, gasping for air and for life. The camera zoomed in on her wounds, the blood pooling around her. So much blood. She heard a voice speak gently, almost tenderly to the dying woman.

"Jackson Gallo sends his regards." Ama gasped in horror as the man stabbed Inca one last time, leaving the knife on the floor next to her body. Then the video ended.

Ama didn't even realize she was screaming until Trevor and Dustin burst into the room, and she collapsed to the ground, sobbing.

RAFF WATCHED the video over and over again, his heart shattering. Enda and his security team had told him about it, and Raff had demanded they send it to him immediately. Enda had cautioned him. "Brother ...don't watch it. Please. I can't imagine anything worse than seeing the woman you love attacked like this. It's horrific."

"Inca had to live it. *Live* it, Enda, not just watch it. I have to do this; there maybe something, or someone I might recognize. You forget I know most people, good or bad, in Naples and Sorrento. This is my home. If they're locals, I'll know it."

After failing to dissuade him, Enda sent the video over, and Raff had watched it. The first time, the shock of it had been ice in his veins. The pain on his beloved Inca's face—the disbelief that this was happening to her *again*. The knife slicing through the white cotton of her dress, the deep claret red of her blood spreading across it. The absolute cruelty of the man who was stabbing her.

He watched it again and again, trying to get used to the horror of it. When he realized that would never happen, he took himself out of the role of husband and tried to focus as an investigator. When the man spoke at the end, Raff heard the accent of the region. Good. That was something he had been right about—they *were* local. In his old life, before Inca, Raff had opened nightclubs, and had enough underworld contacts that he could show this to them and hope against hope they would recognize someone. His contacts would know he wasn't about to go to the police with that information. Raffaelo Winter had every intention of getting everything they knew about Jackson, and then, without hesitation, he would make them feel the pain they had inflicted on Inca tenfold.

INCA KNEW something was wrong when she woke after napping all afternoon. Her body felt heavy, almost as if it was waterlogged. Her belly screamed with pain, and she felt hot. Too hot for this air-conditioned room. She leaned over, reaching for the call button, then felt herself slip and roll. She slammed onto the floor with a moan and then all was darkness.

AMA WOKE in Enda's arms as the phone rang loudly. Enda groaned and rolled over to answer it as Ama glanced at the clock. No news is good at three a.m., she thought and sat up. Enda was rubbing his eyes.

"Yeah? Oh, hey, Raff ...what? Oh god ...how? When? Jesus ...what does the surgeon say?"

Ama's heart caught in her throat. It had to be Inca ...*Jesus*. Ama closed her eyes. *Jackson, you fucking bastard. Why didn't you just kill me?*

She waited for him to finish the call. He looked shattered. "Inca was bleeding internally. They took her back into surgery four hours ago and they're still operating. They can't stop the bleeding. Raff is ... well, you can guess."

Ama dipped her head into her hands and gave a sob. "This is the end, Enda. I've had enough. We need to draw Jackson out. We need to end this."

"I agree." Enda wrapped his arms around her. "Call me selfish or call me a terrible friend, but I never want to have to make that call about you, Ama. And I'm terrified that you'll do something stupidly selfless and get yourself killed."

Ama cried silent tears. "What if he does that to Selima? I cannot live with that, Enda."

"We'll figure something out, baby."

"How?"

But he didn't have an answer for her.

4

PART FOUR

R aff was waiting in the relatives' room with Gajendra and Omar. His phone bleeped and he checked it, relieved at something to do. It was a message from one of his contacts.

Yes. I know these men. Call me back when you can. I hope your lovely Inca pulls through.

If Raff hadn't been so gut-wrenchingly terrified right at that moment, he would have punched the air. Finally, a lead.

The surgeon, exhausted and tired, pushed his way into the room, and Raff tried not to see the blood on his scrubs. Inca's blood. The doctor nodded at him.

"She's stable. We found the bleed; we had thought her spleen hadn't been damaged initially, but that was where the bleed was."

"Will she be okay?" That was Omar; Raff was too relieved to speak.

The doctor hesitated. "We've stabilized her. That's as much information I can confirm. I'm hopeful. Let's say that. You can see her in the morning, Mr. Winter. Until then, I suggest you go home and get some rest."

. . .

Raff, of course, went straight to the home of his contact, where he found out the names of the men who had attacked Inca and could finally see a way to fight for the woman he loved.

Enda put down the phone in frustration and Ama rubbed his back. "What is it?"

"I have to go to New York for the day. The business goes on, even if we're out of action, and I can't ask Raff to leave Inca's bedside right now."

Ama hugged him. "Of course you can't. I have Trevor and Dustin, the silent twins. You go, baby. We can't let this whole thing stop our lives entirely."

Enda kissed her. "Have I told you I love you today?"

Ama grinned. "Well, no, but you certainly *showed* me. And, if you like, you can show me again before I go to work." She lay back, still naked from the shower, and Enda grinned, covering her body with his and hitching her legs around his waist.

"Is that right, *Bella*?"

Ama grinned and sighed happily as she felt his cock begin to swell, pressing hard against her thigh. "Put that in me, Gallo."

"Such a nag," Enda chuckled and thrust his cock deep into her, making her gasp. In moments like these, Ama pretended that the rest of the world went away and that she and Enda were the only two people alive.

They made love slowly, until Enda brought her to a shattering orgasm. She was still glowing when she walked into her office an hour and a half later. Lena grinned at her.

"You look radiant, boss. Anything to do with that gorgeous man of yours?"

Ama grinned, but they were soon bogged down in work. Enda called her as he was about to catch his flight.

"Are you sure you'll be okay? I'll be back around ten tonight."

Ama smiled down the phone. "Honestly, baby, I'm fine. We have a ton of work, so I might be working late myself."

. . .

AS IT TURNED OUT, she was right. The paperwork involved in her handing over her classes to the new teacher which kept her busy all day, and she blinked up at Lena as she came into the office.

"Lena, go home. I got this."

Lena shook her head. "Nah, you stay, I stay. I thought I might skip out and get some coffee for us and Trevor and Dustin. Maybe a sandwich?"

"God, that sounds good. Are you sure you don't mind?"

Lena grinned. "Not at all."

Ama grabbed her purse. "At least let me give you some money."

"Don't worry about it. Be right back. Ham and turkey on rye, right?"

"You're an angel."

Lena gave her a strange smile, then left. Ama pondered her expression for a moment, then shrugged and went back to her work.

SHE WAS SO ABSORBED in what she was doing, that when Lens brought the food and coffee back, she forgot about the drink until it was cold. She picked idly at the sandwich.

"Isn't it good?"

She looked up to see Lena at the door. "No, it's lovely, Lena. Sorry. I got distracted. Did you eat?"

Lena nodded. "I'll put that coffee in a microwave if you like? Reheat it?"

Ama glanced at the cold coffee cup and wrinkled her nose. "No, it's okay. It's never the same. Sorry for forgetting about it."

Lena shrugged. "It's no problem." She hesitated at the door and Ama smiled at her ruefully.

"Seriously, Lena, you should go home. I'm almost done here."

"Then I'll wait." She went out of the door and Ama frowned. Lena was acting ...weirdly? Was that the right word? Usually her younger friend would be out of the door as soon as office hours were over, ready to party all night with her friends. Ama didn't know how she had the energy to do that and still be early for work every morning.

Ama stood and stretched her aching body. The two glass walls of her office, which looked over the conservatory's atrium, reflected her own image back at her now that the atrium was in darkness.

A thump came from outside of her office, and she glanced around, expecting Lena to poke her head around the door and apologize for dropping something. Instead, she heard a muffled cry and darted to the door. Tugging it open, she saw a masked man grabbing Lena.

"Hey!" Anger and adrenaline rushed through Ama as she went to help her friend, wondering where the hell Trevor and Dustin were. She body-slammed the guy, who was twice her size, and he dropped Lena, but grabbed Ama and tackled her, shoving her back into her office.

Ama staggered back, and the man was on her, driving his fist into her stomach. Ama couldn't get her breath and Lena attacked the man from behind as Ama tried to stand.

The man knocked Lena across her desk, and as Ama rushed at him, he grabbed her and slammed her down onto her desk.

Amalia kicked him hard in the balls and the man went down. Ama slid from the desk and ran to help Lena. She almost made it. As Lena screamed, Ama was grabbed from behind.

"No! Don't hurt her!"

But her attacker threw Ama full-force through the plate glass window. The glass shattered and Ama slumped to the floor.

Pain. So much pain.

Her attacker rolled her over, and Amalia realized she had been impaled on a shard of glass which now protruded from her side. She felt faint. Her attacker gave what sounded like a laugh and yanked the glass out of her. More pain. But she couldn't scream or move. Then she heard Lena screaming. "No! No! Don't, please don't. I did what you asked me to do!"

Ama gave a gasp, pushing herself up into a sitting position just as the man drew the lethal edge of the glass across Lena's throat. Ama screamed at him.

"No!"

But it was too late. Lena's throat split open and she clutched at it as it began to gush blood. She looked at Ama, her eyes huge with terror and sorrow. "I'm sorry," she croaked, and then slumped to the ground, pumping red, hot blood onto the floor. Ama tried to move, but the pain of the wound in her side made her struggle and her attacker easily picked her up. As he threw her over his shoulder, she caught a glance of Trevor and Dustin slumped outside the office. Were they dead? There was no one else in the conservatory this late, no one to know she was being taken. She screamed and yelled, but then her assailant slammed her head against the wall and knocked her out.

THE NEWS BROKE as Enda was driving back from the airport and he nearly crashed the car. "No, no, please ..."

All the radio report said was, "Murder at the San Francisco Conservatory of Music ...two young women attacked. One has been confirmed dead. The other is missing ..."

He knew instantly. *Ama.* Jackson had followed through on his threats. As he turned towards the conservatory, he strained to hear the radio through the roaring of blood in his ears. *Please no ...*

His cell phone buzzed loudly and he pressed the hands-free. "Gallo."

"Enda, it's me." Olivier. "Ama's missing. Have you heard about the killing?"

"Yeah," Enda said, relief flooding through him. Missing. Not dead. "Ama's been taken?"

"Yeah. Jackson had someone on the inside, we think. Ama's assistant. Ama's security detail was drugged. They told us the assistant went out for coffee, as they were working late. The two bodyguards drank theirs, but they found Ama's coffee cup still full. Look, where are you?"

"I'm on my way to the conservatory."

"Don't go there. Come home. The F.B.I. are all over the scene and you being there will complicate things. The security guys are being checked out in the hospital, but they're coming here after. We'll coordinate the search for Ama and Selima from here."

Enda pulled the car over to the side of the road and stopped. He hesitated for a moment. "He'll kill her, Olivier. He'll kill them both."

He heard Olivier sigh. "Not necessarily, Enda. Ama's a smart girl. She'll know to play up to his fantasies. To convince him she's ready to be his. If he falls for that...who knows what Ama can make happen. We have to believe in her now."

Enda nodded, closing his eyes. "I do. I believe in her. But I can't stay here doing nothing."

"I know. Come home, brother, and we'll get on it tonight."

RAFF STROKED his wife's hair away from her face. Hours of surgery had saved her again, but it had drained her, and she had been sleeping on and off for a few days now, barely able to hold a conversation. A worried Raff asked the doctor about the possibility Inca may have suffered brain damage, but the doctor reassured him that wasn't what was going on.

"She's just exhausted, Raffaelo, and in my opinion, she's probably rocking back from the assault. I've been worried that she hadn't seemed to process what happened, and I think this is that. PTSD is common in victims of assault, and especially with Inca's past, this doesn't surprise me. She'll rally, I promise. In the meantime, Psych will help her."

Raffaelo had been relieved it was something they could handle together. It killed him that Inca had been targeted yet again; how much was one woman supposed to take?

Stella tapped him on the shoulder as she came to visit Inca. Raff smiled at her. "Thank you, Stella. It's good of you to come."

Stella nodded. "It's my pleasure. Why don't you go home and get some rest?"

Raff looked back at Inca. She was sound asleep again, her breathing regular. "I will, I think. Call me if you need anything."

HE WAS ALMOST home before the call came. "Raff ...I have them."

Raff's adrenaline spiked. It was his underworld contact. "Where?"

The contact named an abandoned warehouse outside the city. "You're sure it's them?"

"Oh, yeah."

Raff's jaw clenched. "I'll be right there."

As he drove out of the city, he tried to stay calm and remind himself that these men might have information that could help them find Ama and Selima. That he, Raff, could ruin everything by killing them. Because, right now, that's all he wanted to do—rip the bastard who had stabbed his beloved Inca limb from limb with his bare hands and smash the brains of the man who had held her, making her helpless to resist.

You're not helping yourself here, buddy. But he couldn't help remember the terror in his wife's eyes as these men tried to kill her.

When he reached the warehouse, he sat in his car for a few moments, trying to steady his nerves. Como, his contact, came out to see him. "Hey."

Raff nodded. "Hey. Thanks for doing this."

Como half-smiled. "This scum hurt your lovely girl. It's my pleasure."

Raff followed him into the warehouse. The two attackers were on their knees, bruised and bloodied. Como's men had obviously beaten them. Raff didn't care. His eyes fixed on the man who had knifed Inca so mercilessly. The man stared back and smirked.

"Well, if it isn't the whore's husband."

Raff's fist smashed into the man's jaw a second later, his temper unleashed. He beat the man almost to unconsciousness before Como pulled him back. Como bent his mouth to Raff's ear.

"My friend ...stop now. Look at his accomplice ...he's scared. He'll talk."

Raff nursed his battered hand and stepped away from the coughing and breathless man on the floor. He looked at the accomplice, who turned wide, terrified eyes on him.

"Please," said the man, "I'm sorry. I'm sorry I helped him ...I promise you, I thought he was going to torment her ...I didn't see the knife."

Como made a disgusted noise. "Filthy liar."

Raff took a step toward the man and he cringed backward. Como's guard kicked him in the small of his back and he groaned. "I swear, friend, I didn't know..."

"...Who paid you?" Raff said in a grim tone. "And don't lie."

"Jackson Gallo. That's what he," he jerked his head towards his injured companion, "told me. He told me Gallo said he needed a distraction so he could send a message to his ex-wife. We were supposed to go kidnap your lady. That's what he told me ...he told me to grab her and hold her arms behind her. He had a camera. Said Gallo wanted to see her scared. What he meant was ...he wanted to see her die. When he stabbed her ...I panicked. Thought if I did anything, he'd kill me too and take the money for himself. I'm sorry about her. I am."

The man was jabbering now, and Raff felt pain shoot through him at his words. So, needless. So, cruel. He turned back to the stabber. "You. Talk, now. Anything. And I'll think about sparing your life."

The man spat blood on the ground. "I don't know anything. Except what he just said. Gallo wanted her killed. Said it sent a message to not fuck with him. I asked him why he didn't do it himself. He told me he couldn't leave the States—that he was in 'seclusion.' That's the word he used."

Raff chewed his lip. "Was this a phone call or video call?"

"Video."

"You record it?"

The man shook his head. His nose was streaming blood. "No."

Raff sighed in frustration. "Tell me about where he was calling from. The room. What was outside the windows? What was the room like?"

The man hesitated. "I got the impression it was ...I mean, there were no windows that I could see and his voice sounded echoey. If I had to guess, I would say it was underground."

Raff studied the man's eyes. He had no reason to lie now; he faced almost certain death the minute Raffaelo gave the order. Even a hardened criminal like this man knew the only way to save himself was by helping them.

Raff turned away and walked back to Como. The other man leaned into him. "What do you want to be done with them?"

Raff didn't answer, struggling with his morality, and Como saw this. "Raff, whatever you need ...we'll deal with it. There need not be any link to you. Let me deal with them."

Raff bowed his head and rubbed his eyes. It would be so easy to just let Como kill them and deal with the bodies. But Raff knew of old how much the weight of responsibility would weigh on him. He'd had to kill before to save Inca's life, and it hadn't sat well with him, although he wouldn't change a thing. Knox Westerwick had been stabbing Inca when Raff had killed him. This was a different situation.

He looked at Como. "No. They might know more. Give them to the police."

"Are you sure?"

Raff nodded. "Very. Too much blood has been spilled already. They can go to jail."

HE KNEW he had made the right decision for himself, for Inca, and for Amalia. Any information was critical now, and as he drove back to the hospital, he called Enda and relayed the information he had discovered. A tired, shattered-sounding Enda thanked him.

"Is there any news, Enda? Anything?"

"Nothing as yet, Raff. But this will help ...we know now they are in California somewhere. If your contact is right and they're somewhere underground, it narrows things down, assuming there's a record of it somewhere."

Raff heard the desolation in his friend's voice. "I've been there, Enda. I know what it's like. We'll find them, I promise."

Enda gave a strangled sob. "God, I hope so ... I don't know what I'll do if we don't."

AMA'S HEAD was screaming with pain, and for a long moment, she debated whether or not to open her eyes at all. Her mind was fuzzy, her chest felt tight, and she became aware of her wrists being tied, plastic biting into the skin. Her mouth was tinder-dry, and she couldn't get a sense of time or place.

She opened her eyes. There was a harsh strip light above her and it made her eyes water. She blinked rapidly, then saw him. Jackson.

"Hello, my darling."

Ama struggled into a sitting position and saw she was in a cell-type room, with gray concrete walls and no windows. "Where's my sister?"

Jackson smiled. "Safe. Her room is significantly more comfortable than this one. If you're good, I'll consider putting you together."

Ama's chest tightened even further. "You have me now, Jackson. Let her go. Please." Everything inside her rebelled against begging him, but for Selima's safety, she would do anything.

Jackson laughed. "Really? You think it's that easy?"

He came to sit next to her. "Now, I'm going to untie you. If you try anything, my men will torture Selima before they kill her. Do you understand?"

Ama nodded and Jackson pulled out a knife. He cut the plastic ties and Ama rubbed her wrists in relief, eyeing the blade Jackson held. He saw her watching it and grinned. "Yep. I don't even need to tell you that this will end up in your gorgeous body if you even think about escaping, do I?"

"What do you want from me, Jackson?"

He leaned over and crushed his lips against hers before answering her. "My wife. That's not too much to ask, is it?"

"So why keep Selima? Please, Jackson, I'll do whatever you want. Just let her go."

Jackson studied her. "Prove to me you can be a good, obedient wife and I'll consider it. I promise you that. But you need to be my wife in every way, Ama. Every way. Do you understand?"

Ama closed her eyes and nodded. *God, Enda ...forgive me.* She felt Jackson's fingers unbuttoning her dress and felt the cold air on her bare skin as he undressed her. She took her mind out of the moment as he fixed his mouth on her breasts and her belly. *Pretend it's not him,* she told herself over and over. She wanted to conjure a good memory of her and Enda, but then pushed that thought away. She didn't want to forever link this rape—and that was what it was—to the glorious lovemaking she and Enda shared.

As Jackson pulled her legs around him and thrust into her, a tear slid down Ama's face. If it weren't for Selima, she would have rather died than give in to the repellent man inside her now. Jackson fucked her, grunting and shouting her name so loudly, she wondered with a pang if, wherever Selima was, she heard it and knew what was happening.

That hurt the most. As Jackson finished, Ama could not help but burst into tears. Jackson grinned. "Yeah, cry all you want. Next time, I expect you to at least act like you enjoy it. If you do, I'll take you to your sister, but, by god, Ama, you better give the performance of your life."

ENDA COULDN'T SLEEP. He was staying with Olivier, and his brother did everything to help Enda feel positive and hopeful. But even though he adored Olivier, his brother couldn't lift the black cloud that stayed with him at all times. Enda missed Ama—her presence, her voice, her laugh, and her scent. He hated that he woke up alone. Now, in the early morning hours, he lay on his back and looked over to 'her' side of the bed. He pictured her sleeping on her stomach, her eyes closed, the thick, dark lashes sweeping her cheeks. Her green eyes opening sleepily, but softening when she saw him.

"Hello, baby."

He would lean over and brush his lips against hers, then make her laugh by rubbing his stubbly chin against hers. She would stretch that heavenly body as he moved across the bed, his cock already straining and engorged for her, and she would open her arms to him, her legs winding around his hips as he slid into her velvety, wet cunt. They would make love slowly, savoring every sensation that rippled through them both, not caring about morning breath, just gazing at each other. Love. Such pure love. As they became more excited and his thrusts became harder, faster, and deeper, he would hear her gasps for air. When she came, back arching, her belly against his, her head thrown back, her pink lips parted as she gave a moan of release.

Ama ...

The sorrow inside him was crushing him, and Enda got out of bed and dressed. He couldn't just sit here and wait for the police to show up and tell him they'd found her body. Even if Olivier was right and Ama knew how to manipulate Jackson, the thought of what she might have to do killed Enda.

He crept out of the house and got into his car. The police said the old Gallo mansion had been gutted in the fire; he was going to go there and see if he could find any clue, anything at all, left in the ashes of the place to tell him where Jackson was holding Ama.

"No! No! Don't. Please don't. I did what you asked me to do!"

Ama woke with a start. Lena ...they'd killed her, but what had she meant by, '*I did what you asked me to do?*' Was she in on the kidnapping? Ama felt sick, dashed to the little toilet in the corner of the room, and threw up and up until she collapsed, exhausted, onto the floor. For the first time, she noticed a small camera high in the corner of the room, trained on the bed. He was watching her. Ama's skin began to crawl. How the hell was she going to escape him? More importantly, how was she going to protect Selima from him?

Ama winced now. The wound in her side from the glass at the conservatory had been patched up by whomever had brought her back to Jackson, but the dressing felt heavy. She eased it off and moaned. The wound had been stitched, but the skin around it looked angry and red. Infection. Fuck. If blood poisoning killed her, Jackson would have no reason to release Selima or even keep her alive. Ama knew, with a sinking heart, she would have to ask him for help. She stumbled over to where the camera was pointing and indicated her wound to it.

"It's infected," she said, not knowing if the room was bugged or if anyone could hear her. "I need antibiotics."

She sat back down on the bed, feeling feverish and sick. Ten minutes later, the door unlocked, and Jackson entered, followed by a smaller, nervous-looking man.

"This is Dr. Harris," Jackson said shortly. "He's here to help you."

Ama nodded and tried to smile at the doctor. "My wound is infected."

Dr. Harris sighed and looked at Jackson. "I told you, Mr. Gallo. That wound is deep. I tried my best, but I'm not a surgeon. She needs to be in the hospital."

Jackson's face was blank. "Not going to happen. Dr. Harris, I assume you realize what will happen if Ama dies of this infection?"

The doctor looked sick, but nodded. "I will have to take some blood, though. I will try to get them processed quickly and anonymously. In the meantime, I'll clean up the wound and give Mrs. Gallo some antibiotics."

"You do that."

While he worked, Ama looked at Jackson. It had been three days since that first time they had slept together, and Jackson had demanded sex multiple times a day ever since. Ama had tried to act as if she enjoyed it, while dying inside, and Jackson had responded. He'd brought her extra blankets and pillows, extra food and drink, and some books. She wondered if, now, she could ask for the thing she wanted most.

"Jackson ...may I see my sister, please? Even for five minutes? I'll ...make you happy later." She flushed scarlet as the doctor gave her a strange look, but Jackson nodded.

"Fine. Five minutes."

She was locked up alone while Jackson took the doctor out, then he returned to her. He tied her hands behind her back. "Just in case you decided suicide is an option and try to attack me," he said. "I'll untie them when you're with Selima. You can have an hour with her today, but I expect you to be ready for me with a smile on your face this evening. Understand?"

Ama nodded, nothing but the excitement at seeing her sister in her mind. Jackson led her through the corridors of the facility. Ama couldn't see any windows anywhere and quickly realized they were underground. The thought made her miserable. How the hell was anyone supposed to find them?

As they walked, the corridors began to look more polished, and by the time they reached Selima's room, they could have been in a four-star hotel. Jackson opened the door, and Selima turned, the shock on her face when she saw Ama obvious.

"Ama!" Selima burst into noisy tears as Jackson untied Ama's hands and left the room. Both of the sisters heard the lock click, then they were in each other's arms.

"I can't believe he's got you here," Selima said. "What happened?"

"He had someone on the inside, I think. God, it's good to see you, but I wish I weren't, if you know what I mean. How are you? Has Jackson ...?"

She couldn't get the words out, and Selima, seeing her distress, shook her head. "No. He hasn't touched me, I promise." She looked bleak. "He killed Chase, Ama. He killed my boyfriend."

Ama shook her head. "No. Chase is alive, Selima. I swear. He's in a bad way, yes, but he's a fighter, and god, he loves you. He's a great guy."

Selima's tears returned, and Ama hugged her while she cried with relief. "Oh, thank god. Thank god."

Ama buried her own tears in Selima's hair. "I'm so sorry, boo, about all of this. It's my fault. I should never have married him ...we could have found another way to get you away from that disgusting ex of yours."

Selima sniffed back her tears and wiped her eyes. "You know that's not true. He would have killed me rather than let me go if Omar's men hadn't made sure he couldn't find me."

"God," Ama said, fierce now. "What the fuck is wrong with these men? We're not objects to own, assholes!"

She yelled it out loud, and Selima smiled. "That's more like it." She sighed. "I'm glad Chase is okay. At least no one else got hurt."

She must have seen something in Ama's face, then, because she paled. "Who?"

Ama hesitated. "Inca. Jackson had her attacked. She almost didn't make it."

Selima looked sick. "Inca? Why the hell?"

Ama's mouth hitched up in a small smile. "Jackson doesn't like it when beautiful women piss him off and treat him like a child. He is that petty and that dangerous. He hired two men to stab Inca to death and it's a miracle she survived ...again."

"She's okay?"

"I wouldn't say that, but she's out of danger. I think, anyway. I've been here for three days and I'm not sure how long I was unconscious."

She told Selima of the circumstances of her abduction, and then her confusion about Lena's involvement. Selima listened with a grim expression on her face.

"That fucking bitch," she spat. "I don't think there's any doubt, Ama. That two-faced ..."

"They killed her, Selima," Ama's voice broke. "In front of me. He slashed her throat, and I saw her die. She's been my assistant for years ...I don't know why she would have done this. Until I know the reason, I can't condemn her ...I just can't."

Selima hugged her sister tightly. "Right. I know. I'm sorry." She sighed. "Look, it's my own fault I'm here. Enda wanted me to have protection, but that night, I just wanted to be alone with Chase, so I gave them the slip. Stupidly. Chase was shot and I was taken. If I had just ..."

"I think we can go round and round on what we both *should have* done, but the person to blame for all of this is Jackson."

Selima studied her sister. "He's making you sleep with him, isn't he?"

Ama nodded. "It's a small price to pay for your safety."

Selima gagged and dashed into the small bathroom of her suite. Ama, nauseated too, followed her, looking around the small room. No windows. Ama was beginning to feel claustrophobic. "We're underground, aren't we?"

Selima nodded. "Yes." She glanced up at the camera and mic above them, then grabbed Ama's hand, leaning into hug her to hide what she was doing. She traced a word onto Ama's palm, just like they had when they were young and keeping secrets from their parents.

Fresno.

Ama was shocked. God, they were so close to home ... She opened her mouth to ask a question, but Selima shook her head. *Right.* They were being watched.

For the rest of the hour, they lay together on Selima's bed and talked about neutral things ...food and their uncle's house in Hyderabad where they had spent many happy summers growing up. Ama didn't talk about Italy, or Enda, or their life there. She picked up from Selima to keep all their discussion's neutral and inoffensive. Maybe if Ama 'behaved,' they would be allowed to stay together more often. Maybe even permanently. If they could spend the night together, when the lights were out they could communicate via their childish language and figure a way out.

LATER, the guards took her back to a different suite, not too far from Selima's, which was again like a hotel room. On the bed was a box containing a note, some expensive-looking lingerie, and a beautiful dark red evening dress. Ama read the note.

. . .

BATHE AND CHANGE *into these items. Tonight, we will dine in your new suite, and then you will show me how grateful you are. If you please me, we will talk about your living arrangements and those of your sister.*

AMA WANTED TO CRY. She closed her eyes and sat on the bed. Was this actually happening? Forced to have sex with a man and pretend it was all she wanted in exchange for the lives of those she loved. Really, how did Jackson expect all this to turn out? It was then she realized— or rather, acknowledged—what she already knew. She, Ama, wasn't *meant* to get out of this alive. Jackson would make her subservient to him until he grew tired of her, and then he would kill her and move on to his next obsession.

In that case, she thought fiercely, *I will make sure Selima gets home, and I will do anything to make that happen. And if I'm destined to die ...I will make damn sure Jackson comes with me.*

She went into the bathroom of the suite and ran the water into the tub. A selection of toiletries were lined up. She had to admit that, when she stepped into the warm water, it was a relief to be clean again. On the countertop were some packages of new underwear and fresh dressings for her wound.

She lay back in the water and let her mind drift to a happy memory. Back in their villa in Italy, their own tub was a vast iron antique that took a half hour to fill, but was the most comfortable she'd ever been in. She and Enda would soak there, kissing and talking as the evening moved into night. Often their lovemaking would begin in the tub.

THE NIGHT she remembered what happened a few months back. Enda had been late home from work and Ama had been composing a new suite for her students to study when she returned to work. She had forgotten the time, and it was only when she looked up that she had realized it was past eight o'clock. As she always switched her phone off when composing, she'd checked her messages and realized she had missed a call from Enda. She'd called him back.

"*Ciao, Bella.*"

She'd grinned. "Hello, gorgeous. I'm sorry I missed your call. I was writing."

"I thought you might be. Listen, I just called to say I'd be late and I wondered if I should pick up a pizza for dinner?"

"As long as we can eat it in bed."

Enda had laughed. "That's what I was hoping. God, what a day."

"Good or bad?"

"Good, but busy. Raff and I might have a track on some investors who are interested in the music schools."

"Sounds fun."

"Ha," Enda had chuckled, "Fun will be the building of the schools. This is the boring, but worthwhile part. How's the writing going?"

"Okay ...I'm not overly happy yet, but it's getting there. Where are you now?"

"Outside Lucio's," he'd said, mentioning their favorite pizza place.

"Good, so you're on your way home."

"I'll be there in a few, *cara mia.*"

She'd met him at the front door, wearing only one of his white shirts. He'd grinned as he'd carried the pizza inside, stopping to kiss her. "I'm the luckiest man alive."

"You bet you are."

The pizza had gotten cold, while they were kissing, they'd tumbled to the floor, Ama stripping his jacket and tie off and Enda's hands pushing his short from her beautiful bod. He'd pinned her down on the cold, hard tile of the lobby and taken her there, Ama screaming his name as his cock plowed into her, her hips burned as he pressed them further apart.

Afterward, they'd eaten pizza in bed and then soaked in the bath. It hadn't been long until Ama, who had been laying back against

Enda's chest, turned and straddled him in the water, stroking his cock and then impaling herself on it. She'd gazed at her lover, his dark curls wet and sticking to his face, his smile and his green eyes so full of love for her. God, he was glorious.

"I want to marry you, Enda Gallo. Someday. When I'm free from Jackson and when all of this is over. No big ceremony. Just you and me on a remote island, away from everybody else. It doesn't even have to be legal—just enough that you know how much I love you and how much I will love you for as long as I live ..."

His arms had tightened around her, and his kiss had been fierce and full of passion. "I can't wait, Amalia, my *Principessa*. As far as I'm concerned, I'm already your husband."

IF ONLY THAT WERE TRUE, Ama thought miserably as she dressed for a 'romantic' dinner with the monster who was legally her husband. She pulled on the lingerie he had bought her absentmindedly, then changed the dressing on her wound. She hoped the antibiotics would kick in soon. At least a decent meal would do her good.

SHE WAS ready when Jackson arrived, followed by one of his guards pushing in a trolley loaded with covered plates. The guard left immediately, and Jackson locked the door.

He looked her up and down. "You look beautiful, darling."

Ama gave him a half-smile, trying to make it look genuine. "The dress is lovely. Thank you, Jackson."

He beamed. "See how much nicer things are when we are civil? Please sit, Ama, and I will serve."

She sat down obediently, and Jackson put a covered plate in front of her. He made a flourish as he pulled the cover off, but then laughed—almost a giggle, like a naughty school boy. A small handgun sat on the plate. "Oh, silly me, wrong plate." He leaned in so his face was next to hers and Ama tried not to cringe away from him. "That's what I'll use on you if you do anything—anything—to displease me during this dinner, darling. You'll get three and your sister will get the other three. Now, can you promise me we will have a good time tonight?"

"Yes."

"Louder."

She met his gaze. "*Yes,* Jackson." *You had better pray I don't get my hands on that gun, Jackson, because if I do, you'll wish you'd never been born.* She gave him a wide smile and kissed him lightly.

Jackson drew back, smiling. "Good." He tucked the gun into the back of his waistband and swapped the plates over. This time, when he lifted the cover, Ama nearly swooned at the smell of the food underneath. A perfectly cooked T-bone steak oozing with garlic butter, a baked potato, and some lightly-cooked vegetables. Despite her fear and anger, Ama's mouth filled with saliva. Jackson seemed pleased at her reaction. He sat at the opposite end of the table while they ate, the handgun resting next to his hand.

The food was good and Ama suddenly realized she was starving. Jackson poured them some red wine and Ama sipped it. She wondered if she should, given the tablets the doctor had sent for her, but she would do anything to get through this.

She started to feel strange as they finished their entrees. Her head was swirling. Too much wine? As she picked at the fruit salad Jackson had given her for dessert, she started to feel out of it completely. *Maybe I'm just exhausted,* she thought, but her skin felt like it was on fire.

Jackson was watching her carefully. "Something wrong, darling?" His grin was wide.

Ama started to stand, knocking her wine glass to the floor. "Jackson ...did you put something in my drink?"

He laughed. "Just a little something to relax you, Ama. Don't worry, it won't harm you. Just make things go a little smoother between us."

Her vision was blurry. "Jackson ...I don't feel so good ..."

She stumbled toward the bathroom, but Jackson caught her in his arms. "It's okay, darling. Just relax into it."

She felt herself being carried to the bed, then her skin felt cool as Jackson peeled the dress from her. "Just pretend I'm my bastard brother, Ama ..." His voice sounded far away and her limbs felt like liquid.

When Jackson's cock thrust into her, she was barely conscious, but still, the rocking motion and the smell of him made her want to throw up. *Play your role. Don't forget he holds all the cards here. Say his name.*

"Jackson," she whispered and heard his satisfied chuckle.

"Good, good ...now, Ama, this is only the beginning of the evening. I have a surprise for you."

Ama was so out of it, by the time Jackson had cum, she barely felt him pull her up into his arms and carry her from the room, draped only in the bed sheet. He strode down the hallway with her, and before Ama could try and see where he was taking her, he was walking into a darkened room. "We're going to have some different kind of fun tonight, my darling."

He set her down onto what felt like a wooden bench, then adjusted the lighting. Ama, blinking to try and wake herself up, felt a jolt of shock go through her. From the ceilings, hung chains with cuffs on the end. A large, wooden bed with stocks and St. Andrew's Cross stood at the other end of the room. On one wall, whips, paddles, restraints, and harnesses hung from hooks. On another, a huge flat screen T.V. On a credenza under the T.V., knives lay out.

Oh god, someone help me.

It was a bondage room, but it had Jackson's twist on it. It wasn't a place of experimentation, of BDSM, or of loving adventure, but a torture chamber. He wanted her humiliated, scared, and in fear of her life. That's what turned Jackson on.

She looked back at him, and his face was alive with desire and triumph.

"Before you left me for the bastard," he said. "I was planning to have this built in our home—after Dad had passed, obviously. Eventually, after the two years were up and you were going to leave me, I would have brought you here for one last time. One last time before I killed you. I was never going to accept you leaving me, Ama. You know that now, right?"

Barely conscious and terrified, she nodded. Jackson took her in his arms. "Now, there are two ways this evening could go. One...you try to enjoy it and make me happy, and you live. Your sister lives. The other ..." He nodded to the case of knives. "I use *all* of them on you. They won't even bother to count the stab wounds, Ama, I swear to you. I'll take my time, and you will know what hell feels like."

"Why?" Ama said now, her voice barely more than a whisper, "Why me? Why all of this just for me? Why did you try and kill Inca too?"

Jackson grinned. "Speaking of which ..."

He grabbed the remote control and on the flat screen, the video of Inca being stabbed played. Ama gave a cry of distress.

"I've watched this over and over again, just enjoying the terror and pain on her beautiful face. The way the knife slides into her belly like butter. The way the blood blooms across her dress."

Jackson looked back at Ama, who was trembling uncontrollably. His eyes were cold and dead, and now Ama saw the madness within. "I wish I had ordered the men I sent to kill Penny to film it too. I didn't even think about it until I ordered the hit on Inca."

He was insane. A monster. A ...Ama didn't have the words for it. But inside her mind, one thought began to fester. *He is insane ...use that. Use it to get Selima released. Use it to save your own life if you can...*

Ama knew what she had to do now. She had to push all her feelings aside and allow Jackson to do what he wanted ...even it meant the worst kind of violation. If it meant getting him to trust her, she would take that risk.

God, Enda, I'm sorry ...I'm trying to fight my way back to you.
Please forgive me.

ENDA HAD NOT FOUND anything in the rubble of his father's home. He'd contacted the forensics team, who had let him examine what little was left of his father and brother's possessions. There were some old photographs, badly burned and warped, a few old letters that Macaulay had written to Olivier and Jackson's mother, receipts, and bills. But there was nothing else. No clues.

Frustrated, he drove into his office. The police knew to find him there, and at least he could coordinate the search from there.

Raffaelo called him just after midday. "Guess what?"

"Tell me."

"We're coming to the States."

Enda was astonished. "Inca's well enough?"

Raff hesitated, then sighed. "Not really, but she is insistent. There's a surgeon over there who might be able to fix some of the scarring. Between us, I think Inca's using that as an excuse. She knows I couldn't say no to her. She is much stronger now and she's not hooked up to any machinery. I negotiated a nurse to come with us, but yes, we're coming to America."

Enda sat down with a bump. "Selfishly, Raff, I can't wait to see you all, but do you really think this is a good idea?"

"Inca and I ...we want to be there for you, Enda. You are my brother, and we can't see you hurting like this."

Enda was so touched he couldn't speak. Raff laughed softly. "We'll be there tomorrow, Enda. Stay strong."

THE NEXT DAY, Enda drove out to the airport to meet their private jet. Inca smiled at him, but he was shocked at how thin and pale she was. Raff hugged him tightly. "We're all together now ...we will find Ama, I swear it."

ENDA INSISTED THAT RAFF, Inca, and Inca's nurse, a sweet woman in her fifties called Giovanna, or 'Vanni,' as Inca already called her, stay with him. "Don't be fooled by that gorgeous face," Inca had warned Enda, as Giovanni giggled, "She rules me with a rod of iron."

Enda marveled again at Inca's ability to draw people to her, even when she was obviously still in a lot of pain. Raff looked older, saddened, and wrecked by what had happened, but Enda watched him rallying, trying to hide his misery.

When Enda got Raff on his own later, Raff admitted he was shattered. "I just feel so damn helpless. Is the answer really locking Inca up in an ivory tower to keep her safe?"

"God, I'm so sorry, Raff. If it's any consolation, I feel exactly the same, man."

Raff nodded. "Of course. Sorry. Look, take me through what you've found out already."

THEY POURED over the maps of California. "We think he planned this down to the most minute detail; wherever his compound is, it is deeply hidden. The places the police and my team have searched all had roads leading to them. Wherever Jackson is, it's out in the wilds somewhere."

Enda gave a short laugh, running his hands through his dark hair. "I've spent days just on Google Earth, just trying to figure out *something*. We're going to have to extend the search, I think."

Raff nodded. "We need new teams, then. People who aren't jaded from searching."

"I agree. And we need to do this in a grid pattern, I think. However much it costs."

"Money isn't an object. You know that. Let's just get them home."

AMA WOKE UP, her limbs stiff. She felt a hand on her arm and skittered away from it in alarm.

"It's me, Ama." Selima. Ama let out a long breath. She was in Selima's room, on top of her bed. Selima poured a cup of water for her.

"They brought you here last night, late. Jackson said we could stay together now. He looked ...weird."

Ama sipped the cold water and closed her eyes. Last night had been the worst, most degrading, most humiliating night of her life, but she couldn't break down. Not with Selima still here. Selima put her arms around her sister.

"Talk to me."

"I can't," Ama whispered. "I never want you to know what happened."

Her words were enough to make Selima start to weep gently. "Oh, no, no, Ama, no ..."

Ama hugged her back tightly before releasing her. "I need to bathe."

Selima helped her undress and tried not to let the horror fill her eyes as she looked at the cuts, welts, and bruises on her sister's body. Ama felt broken, and as she stepped into the tub, she winced as the hot water stung her wounds.

She felt disconnected from herself, completely soulless and empty. Jackson had done things to her which she would not allow herself to think of and would certainly never tell Selima ...or Enda. Jackson was a monster, an aberration of a human, and Ama knew now there was only one way she could save her sister, and that was to sacrifice herself.

After she had bathed, she knocked on the door. The guard opened it. "Tell Jackson I want to see him. Now. I have a proposal for him." The guard nodded and was about to shut the door when Ama stopped. "And tell him to bring his favorite knife."

Selima's eyes opened wide, but Ama shook her head at her. "I know what to do now, Selima. I'm getting you out of here. So, for the next few minutes, when Jackson gets here, I want you to go into that bathroom and give me some space. Don't listen to what I'm saying. Can you do that?"

Selima nodded, her eyes terrified. When Jackson arrived, Selima went into the bathroom. Ama faced her husband.

Jackson studied her and smiled. "You look beautiful."

Ama stared back at him, then dropped her robe. "Am I? Do you like me bruised, cut, and wounded, Jackson?"

He grinned widely. "I think you know the answer to that."

"I do." She walked towards him, naked. "You get off on hurting women; it's what fuels you, yes?"

She grabbed his hand, the one with the knife, and stepped closer so that the tip of the blade pressed against her belly. "Do it, Jackson. You know you want to. Run me through."

Jackson's eyes grew wary and he jerked the knife away from her. "Why would I want to do that ...especially after we discovered new realms of pleasure together last night."

God ...there wasn't a word for how vile he was. "Do you want to do it again?"

"Of course."

"Then here's my proposal. Let my sister go, unharmed. You or one of your goons delivers her to a hospital, in whatever state you like. When I see she's safe on the television, I'll go with you anywhere. I'll do *anything* with you. They need never find us."

Jackson narrowed his eyes. "And what if I don't?"

"Then pick up that knife and kill me now. Because if you think I'm going to let you touch me ever again after last night, after what you did to me, without me getting something in return ..."

His hand shot up and grabbed her throat. "What guarantee do I have that you'll keep your end of the bargain if I let Selima go?"

Ama stared back, her gaze cool. "You don't. But then you get to kill me and jerk off over my dead body. It's a win-win for you."

Jackson was quiet for a long moment. "You know how this will end eventually, don't you, Amalia? Your blood on my hands."

She nodded. "I know."

He released her, and she stepped back, pulling her robe on. Would he go for it? Ama realized she was holding her breath.

Jackson nodded. "I'll think about it."

"Thank you."

WHEN JACKSON HAD GONE, Selima came out of the bathroom, tears streaming down her face. She had obviously been listening.

"I'm not leaving you."

Ama nodded. "Yes, you *are*. Selima, look ...this is the only way. You're my best chance. If you can lead the police here, or at least tell them anything, I might have a chance. Otherwise, last night proved to me one thing: Jackson doesn't intend to let me go alive. Ever. But you do get the chance to live."

Her voice broke, and Selima came to her. "I won't leave you," she repeated through her sobs.

Ama hugged her tightly. "You *have* to ...you have to tell Enda that I love him. That I'll love him forever. Please, Selima ...please do this for me."

A COUPLE OF HOURS LATER, Jackson returned with two guards and the doctor in tow. The doctor gave Ama a strange look, but Jackson didn't notice. "You have a deal, Ama. You," he looked at Selima. "The doctor is here to give you something for the journey. Don't worry. It's just a sedative. Can't have you picking out details to help identify this place. My men will take you to a hospital, where you will ask to talk to the press so that Ama can see you're safe. Say your goodbyes, ladies."

Ama hugged her sobbing sister. "Live well, Selima, for me. Tell Enda I love him and that I don't regret a moment with him."

After a few minutes, Jackson got impatient. "Enough. Doctor!"

The doctor injected Selima and Ama held her hand as she passed out. She looked at the two men. "Please take care of her."

One of them nodded and the other stood stone-faced. Ama kissed her sister's forehead, and the men carried Selima out. Ama was terrified, then, that Jackson would go back on his word and he saw it on her face. "We had an agreement, Ama. Your sister will be safe."

And for some reason, she believed him. She sat down heavily on the bed and felt exhausted. The doctor looked at her and felt her forehead. "You're running a temperature. Maybe I should check your wound out."

Jackson nodded. "I'll give you ten minutes, Doc. Do whatever she needs."

He left them alone. The doctor helped her out of her dress and winced when he saw the new wounds. "I don't have long, but I will take care of these." He leaned in closer. "My dear, I must tell you. I ran the blood tests. There is a slight infection, but nothing that won't be knocked out by the antibiotics. There is something else. You are pregnant, my dear."

INCA, still confined to a wheelchair, asked Vanni to roll her towards Enda's study. When she got there, the two men were still locked in discussion over a map of California. They looked up as she was rolled in.

"Thanks, Vanni," Inca smiled at her nurse, who grinned and went out of the room. Inca waved a couple of photos at Enda. "Enda, these came from the fire-damaged stuff. Can you tell me where they are?"

He took the old, faded, and damaged Polaroid from her and studied it. One showed a field and trees, the sun scorched. The other a set of stepping stones across a small creek. Enda frowned. "I don't know, Inca. Why?"

"I'm thinking—is it somewhere Jackson went as a kid? The photos are old and faded, but I was just wondering if it's somewhere Jackson feels close to, or has good memories of, he might ..." She trailed off as she looked at the skepticism on their faces. "I know. I'm reaching, but, for the love of God, he has to be somewhere."

Raff went to his wife and hugged her. "Any idea is good at this stage, *Bella*. Sorry if we seemed a little off."

Enda nodded. "Agreed. Anything is good now. Olivier will be here soon; we'll ask him if he can tell us anything.

TWO HOURS LATER, Olivier was nodding his head. "Yeah ...this was a place our mom used to take us when she wanted to get us away from all the 'opulence,' as she put it, and let us be normal kids for once. She used to make us fish in the creek and hike through the hills. We always loved those days out; believe it or not, it was the one time that Jackson and I actually got along."

Enda tried not to get too excited. He exchanged a look with Inca. "Where is it?"

"Out in Fresno County, near a place called Humphrey's Station." Olivier finally got it. He looked between the three of them. "Really? You think he could be there?"

"It's a possibility," Enda said. "At this moment, I'll take any lead."

"We have some men in the area, scouring it, and I mean, practically inch-by-inch. There must be some evidence of him being there if we're right."

Suddenly the door burst open and Vanni came in. "Mr. Gallo, please, the television ..."

She was breathless and half-crying. Enda flicked on the tv and they all froze.

Selima Rai, tears pouring down her face, was flanked by two female police officers, begging them all to save her sister.

AMA SAT on the cool bathroom floor, her head in her hands. Pregnant. How? She had been on the pill for months now ...only she had missed the last few days for obvious reasons. Did that mean the baby was Jackson's? God ...

But she couldn't hate the little life inside her, because there was a chance, a very *small* chance that it could be Enda's child. Earlier, before she knew about her pregnancy and after Selima had gone, she had come to terms with the fact that she would probably be killed soon. She accepted it.

But now? She had to try and save herself and the baby. That was evident. She started as Jackson came into the suite and called her name.

"In here. I'll be out in a second."

She flushed the toilet and splashed water on her face. When she went back into the bedroom, Jackson smiled at her. "Time to watch a little T.V., darling."

. . .

IN THE BONDAGE ROOM, where Ama deliberately didn't look at the bed where she had been so hideously violated the night before, Jackson switched on the television. He flicked to the news channel, and when Ama saw her sister's face, safe, with the police, she burst into tears. *Thank god. Thank god …*

She felt Jackson put an arm around her. "Ama …from now on, we will be a happy couple. Together. Tonight, we will be flying to another place, somewhere they will never find us. Thank you for giving me this gift, my love."

Christ, he really is insane, isn't he? A happy couple? Play along, her subconscious told her.

She looked up and smiled at him. "Thank you, Jackson. Thank you for keeping your word."

Jackson kissed her and she forced herself to respond. He pushed her dress away from her shoulders and stripped her, and Ama went along with it, kissing him passionately and freeing his cock from his pants. Clarity had come to her since the doctor told her about the baby, and she'd figured out that this room, this terrible room, was her way out of this place.

That and Jackson's arrogance. She smiled at him. "I want to taste you." She nearly gagged on the words, but Jackson, smiling, nodded and pushed her head down to his lap. Ama took his cock into her mouth. As she teased and sucked him, she flicked her eyes around the room, taking in every chance she had to get an advantage. His rack of knives was the most obvious, but they were over on the other side of the room.

Anything. Anything will do …adrenaline coursed through her body as she realized this was the moment. This was the time.

Jackson grunted and grinned down at her. "That feels so good, baby. So, good. Let me cum in your mouth…"

And as he came, groaning, Ama clenched her jaw and bit down as hard as she could.

· · ·

As soon as Selima confirmed that they had been held somewhere near Fresno, the F.B.I. and Enda, Raffaelo, and Olivier flew out in helicopters to the place where Olivier and Jackson played as kids. Inca had wanted to come, but Raffaelo forbade it, telling her, "No way. I don't want you within a million miles of guns and Jackson Gallo."

She had protested, but gave up when Raffaelo made it clear he was serious. "And besides," Raffaelo told her. "Selima is being brought here. You'll need each other if ...anything goes south." He lowered his voice so Enda couldn't hear him. "Keep away from the news. Obviously the F.B.I. have ordered a news blackout until after the operation, but you never know."

Now, as he sat in the helicopter beside Enda, he could see his friend was beyond anxious. Enda jiggled his legs constantly, staring out of the window as California passed beneath them. But Raffaelo felt optimistic for the first time in days. They had a lead.

As they reached the small, isolated place called Humphrey's Station, an F.B.I. Agent met them. "We've found it. It's buried in the hillside, and we would have missed it, except that we spotted a car coming out of one of the valleys leading to it. A doctor. We picked him up, and he caved and spilled his guts to us. Mr. Gallo, your partner is being held inside. We're concerned that there are many armed guards in there with her, as well as Jackson Gallo. We need to approach this carefully."

Enda could have screamed in frustration. *Just go in there and get her.* But he knew they were right. If Jackson were alerted to the fact they had been found, he would kill Ama and shoot his way out.

Raff put a hand on his shoulder. "We're nearly home, Enda. Stay strong."

.   .   .

JACKSON SCREAMED as Ama's teeth clamped onto his penis. Ama tasted blood, and when she saw him buckle, she released her grip and staggered back away from him, over to where he kept the knives. In horror, she saw that a glass lid had been placed over them and locked.

Fuck.

Jackson was recovering now—as best as he could with only half a penis. Ama had spat him out. Now he was staring at her with murder in his eyes.

But instead of being scared, Ama found herself angry. Furious. Raging. She grabbed whatever she could find and hurled it at him as he lunged at her, ducking out of his grip. She found a paddle in her hand and slammed it into his face. Jackson reeled, but just as Ama thought she might have the upper hand, Jackson grabbed a whip and caught her on her face before looping it around her neck and pulling it tight. Ama choked, twisted, and turned, trying to free herself, but her airways were cut off, and she felt unconsciousness coming. Desperate—giving into the darkness would mean certain death—she grabbed at anything she could. It was a studded harness, leather and heavy. She flung it back, again and again, hoping to catch Jackson in the eye, and when he gave a howl and the whip around her throat eased and fell to the floor, she knew she'd hit her mark. She dived across the bed and threw herself onto the glass-topped credenza, hoping her weight would smash the glass. It cracked, but didn't break.

"You fucking bitch! I'll kill you. I'll kill you!" Jackson was lunging at her again, and in desperation, she plowed her elbow into the glass with all her strength. Both her elbow and the glass smashed, and despite the agonizing pain shooting up her arm, she grabbed what she could—a shard of glass—and as Jackson grabbed her, she lashed out.

Jackson staggered back as Ama was covered in a mist of blood from the gushing wound in his neck. Jackson fell to the floor, his carotid bursting from the pressure of blood escaping the wound.

Ama dropped to her knees, gasping for air and searching for the keys in Jackson's pockets. He grabbed her arm. "I'll kill you ..."

She shook his hand off. "Go to hell, Jackson. Which is where you'll be in a few more seconds, I'm guessing. You're bleeding out, idiot, and no one, *no one,* will mourn you." Her anger was still ruling her as she grabbed a knife from the smashed cabinet. "This is for Selima, for Inca, and for Penny." She slammed the knife into his chest, straight into his heart. Jackson made a gurgling noise in his throat, then his head fell to the side, his eyes staring but unseeing.

Ama sat back, catching her breath. Now what? She had to find the exit, unarmed and facing god knows how many armed guards who would shoot her in a second. She placed a hand on her belly.

"Come on, little one. We've come this far." She grabbed Jackson's keys, unlocked the door, and slipped out of the room into the corridors.

ENDA WATCHED the F.B.I. and the S.W.A.T. team planning and felt a rush of irritation. He knew it wasn't fair, but they had been there hours, and Ama was still in there, the authorities deeming it too risky to go in yet.

"Why? How much more risk can it be for Ama?"

But Raff calmed him down. Now it was getting dark and they were still strategizing. Fuck this. Enda ducked behind the police vehicles and ran around to where they said the entrance was, ducking behind shrubs and trees and moving stealthily in the gloom. At the entrance, he saw a guard outside, patrolling. He padded silently behind the man and took him out with a punch to the temple. The man crumpled silently. Enda grabbed his gun and cold-cocked him again just to make sure he was down. He relieved the guard of his handcuffs and bound his hands behind his back.

"What the fuck are you doing?"

Enda spun around to see a furious Raff behind him. Enda sighed. "Go back, Raff. This is my battle."

"No way."

Enda shook his head. "Don't be stupid ...you and I both know this is a suicide mission. Don't leave Inca a widow."

Raff's face was hard. "No, just give her a coward as a husband. You go in, I go in. That's how this is going to work."

Enda could tell Raff wouldn't shift. "Fine. Stay behind me. We only have one weapon between us."

He unlocked the entrance door and slipped inside, Raff close behind him.

OLIVIER WAS TALKING to the F.B.I. Agent in charge, and now he looked around to bring his brother, and his friend, into the conversation. He couldn't see them anywhere.

Olivier frowned. Where the fuck were they? Then it hit him and he cursed loudly. The F.B.I. Agent looked at him, and Olivier turned his grim-set face toward him.

"Yeah. We may have a problem."

ARMED WITH A KNIFE, Ama staggered through the hallways, her ears on high alert. She had to duck into rooms she didn't know were occupied, and more frustratingly, she seemed to be getting deeper and deeper into the labyrinth of tunnels. She paused in a dark corridor, trying to quell the rising panic. She heard two men approaching and slid back into the darkness.

"What do you think he's doing to her tonight?" The man had a mocking tone to his voice.

"Don't know, but I wouldn't want to be that girl. He's a sick fucking freak. If he didn't pay so well, I'd take him out myself. Poor kid."

"Yeah, right. She looks like a whore."

"Have some respect, asshole."

Ama frowned. They hated Jackson as much as she did. Maybe they would help her ...*no. Don't be stupid. You've just killed their money maker.* When they had passed, she tracked back where they had come from and followed the hallways back past the room where Jackson lay dead, then toward the room where she and Selima were held. Something told her this was the right way. She felt a pain shooting through her—a cramp, or maybe her wound had opened up. She glanced down to see blood soaking her bare skin, remembering she was only clad in her underwear. What a fucked-up situation. She nearly giggled, a hysterical reaction to the circumstances.

"Stop right there, beautiful, or you'll force me to put a bullet in that gorgeous body."

Ama froze. *Shit. Stupid woman. You lost focus.* She turned slowly to see one of the guards aiming his pistol at her. "Put the knife down, sweetheart."

She dropped the knife, raising her hands.

"Where's Jackson?"

Ama swallowed. *No way out now.* "Dead. I killed him. So, do what you want to me. He's dead and I'm fucking glad."

The guard looked surprised, then grinned. "Good. Then maybe I can have some fun with you before I kill you, gorgeous."

He had started to approach her when Ama heard the shot. She felt the rush of air over her head and saw the bullet hit the guard straight in the forehead. He dropped like a stone and Ama spun around ...to see her love, her Enda, his gun still raised. She couldn't believe it. Enda lowered the gun and handed it to Raff, who was smiling at her. Enda walked slowly at first, then as Ama started to run toward him, he started to run too and swept her into his arms. Ama was sobbing now, not caring who heard them. Enda kissed her face and her hair, his voice breaking as he told her he loved her over and over.

"Guys, we have to go. Now." Raff looked apologetic, but Enda nodded. Still carrying Ama, they raced back towards the entrance. As they reached the door, shots rang out, barely missing them, and they threw themselves outside and ran.

Spotlights flooded the area, then, and they blinked in the lights. Chaos ensued. F.B.I. Agents took them to safety, and soon Ama and Enda were in an ambulance racing towards Fresno and a hospital.

. . .

AT THE HOSPITAL, a doctor examined her as Enda went to call Olivier. Ama grabbed the doctor's hand. "I'm pregnant," she whispered," No one knows. Can you tell how far along I am?"

The doctor, a kind looking woman, smiled. "We'll run some tests. Discreetly," she added. "In the meantime, you're going to need a minor surgery to help you heal."

LATER, Enda came back, and they enjoyed some alone time, finally. Enda hugged her tightly. "God, to think I nearly lost you."

Ama relaxed into his arms. "It's over now, baby. We can be happy."

"Damn right."

They sat in companionable silence for a few minutes before Ama looked at him, her eyes serious. "I killed Jackson. Your brother."

"*Half*-brother. And fuck him. The world's a better place."

"Do you think Olivier thinks so?"

Enda swept her hair away from her face. "*Cara mia*, Olivier loves you. You did what you had to do to survive. He knows you did the right thing."

"He's grieving, though?"

Enda nodded. "Just for the idea of a brother, rather than Jackson, I think. But believe me, he's one-hundred percent behind you."

Ama sighed. "I can't wait to get out of here."

"The minute we do, I'm marrying you."

Ama laughed. "Well, you'd better."

"Knock, knock." It was the doctor from earlier, who smiled at her. "We've run the tests."

Ama felt her heartbeat quicken. "How many?" *Months,* she asked silently, and the doctor nodded.

"Three." And she grinned. Ama burst into tears, smiling through them. Enda was utterly confused.

"What's going on?"

The doctor smiled again and left the room, closing the door

behind her. Ama couldn't speak from relief and joy, but finally, when Enda was starting to look worried, she held his face in her hands, her eyes shining, and told him that in six months, he was going to be a father and their life as a family could really begin

THE END

5

HIS BROTHER'S WIFE EXTENDED EPILOGUE

Erotic Romance

By Michelle Love

Amalia Gallo shifted her daughter onto her hip. Serafina, with her caramel skin, bright green eyes, and dark wavy hair to her waist, grinned up at her mom. At two years old, she was merry and loving, and Ama kissed her forehead now, feeling the familiar swell of love as she breathed in her daughter's smell of powder and soap.

"Come on, *Piccolo*. Let's go see everyone."

She took Serafina—Sera, as they called her—out onto the terrace of the villa, where Sera's dad, Enda, greeted them both with a kiss. Their best friends, Raffaelo and Inca, greeted her with smiles, and Inca stole Sera away from her mother immediately, making Ama laugh.

"You wouldn't take her so quickly when she's in a bad mood," she chuckled, and Inca rolled her eyes.

"Don't give me that. This scruffy muppet is a bundle of sunshine." She tickled the little girl, who shrieked with laughter and cuddled her 'aunt.'

Ama sighed happily. In the two-and-a-half years since she'd escaped from and then killed her abusive ex-husband, her life had changed immeasurably. She had made Sorrento her home permanently since her marriage to Enda Gallo—the love of her life and the reason she was still alive. It had been his half-brother, Jackson, to whom Ama had been unhappily married, who had abducted her, and who had tried to kill Inca to teach Ama a lesson and get his revenge on his 'bastard' brother. Jackson was dead now, though, and since the day she had escaped, they had lived happily and safely in Italy.

THEIR FRIENDS WERE there for breakfast, and as the morning sun beat down, they ate fresh fruit and pancakes, Serafina tucking into as many things as her little hands could hold. Ama ate yogurt and fruit and asked Inca about her upcoming fortieth birthday celebration. She couldn't believe her friend would be forty soon. Inca could have easily passed for her early twenties still, but her looming birthday didn't seem to bother her. Raff, her drop-dead gorgeous husband, was in his early fifties and his dark hair was shot through with silver.

"I still haven't decided what I want to do to celebrate it," Inca said. "Raff wants to take me away somewhere remote and paradise-ey—is that a word?"

Ama grinned. "No, but it works."

"So, yeah ...I really don't want a big party or anything. I'd rather just go out for a great meal with you and Enda, and Tommaso and Bo."

"Then that's what we'll do." Ama smiled at her friend. She and Inca had become incredibly close since Ama had moved to Italy and they were now more like sisters than friends. Ama's own sister, Selima, had recently gotten engaged to her American boyfriend, Chase, who was another victim of Jackson's psychopathy. Their wedding didn't have a date yet, but Selima was laid back about the whole thing. "Don't be surprised if we just do it in the Elvis Chapel in Vegas," she had said down the phone one evening, and Ama had laughed.

"That wouldn't surprise me at all."

Her own wedding had been as low key—City Hall in San Francisco, with Selima and Raff as their witnesses. Inca, who had been in a wheelchair because she was recovering from being stabbed, was an honorary flower girl, much to her delight.

AFTER BREAKFAST—AND after Inca had reluctantly given Sera back to her mother—their friends departed and Enda smiled at his wife. "Good way to start the day."

"Isn't it? Now, what shall we do today? I'm assuming you're not working?"

Enda looked a little guilty, and Ama frowned. "Really?"

"Only for an hour, I swear. Just to finalize the details of the opening. One hour, I promise, and then we'll take the munchkin to the beach."

Ama sighed. "Deal. I'll make a picnic."

SERA HELPED her mother as best she could, smearing butter on crusty bread to make sandwiches as her mother chopped and sliced the fillings for them. She grinned at the concentration on her daughter's face. Ama still couldn't believe this adorable little creature was hers.

"Mama?"

"Yes, pooh?"

"Why hasn't Auntie Inca got a 'Fina?" Sera hadn't yet realized that her name wasn't *every* child's name.

"Well, nugget, some people can't have children."

"Why?"

Ama swallowed. God, the inevitable 'why' questions had begun already. "It's to do with ...stuff inside the human body. It's hard to explain. But Auntie Inca loves you very much. She just doesn't want children of her own, and there's nothing wrong or strange about that."

Sera seemed satisfied with that and gave a wide yawn.

"Sleepy, muppet?"

Sera nodded, and Ama lifted her into her arms. "Come on, then. Nap time before we go to the beach."

Settled in her own little bed, Sera fell asleep almost immediately. Ama stroked her daughter's hair back from her face.

She felt Enda's arms snake around her waist and pull her to him. "Nap time?"

She turned in his arms. "Work's done?"

"Work's done." He bent his head to kiss her. "So ...nap time?"

Ama grinned and took his hand. "I think we can find something to do other than sleep ..."

IN THEIR BEDROOM, she set the baby monitor down, and Enda laughed a little. "Remember when we didn't have to keep one ear listening?"

Ama grinned. "Actually, no. Still," she went to him and kissed him, "We were blessed with a child who knows how to nap properly. So, let's not waste any of this time ..."

They kissed passionately as they stripped each other and then climbed onto their bed. Ama straddled her husband as he stroked her breasts and her belly.

"*Bellissimo*," he said in a soft voice, and she grinned, her hands moving to stroke his cock, feeling it quiver and harden under her touch. His fingers gripped her hips as he lifted her so she could take him in. God, this never got old, the feeling of his huge cock filling her and his hands on her body. Ama began to rock her hips, sliding him in and out of her, their hands locked together, their breathing becoming ragged and excited. She saw Enda watching his cock as it moved in and out of her cunt, and soon she too was transfixed by the sight.

"I would love to film this," Enda said. "You're so beautiful, my darling."

Ama grinned. "Maybe we should try new things—not that we need to spice things up—but it could be fun."

Enda nodded. "Are you sure? After what Jackson did to you?"

Ama's smile faltered a little, but then she shook her head. "If anything, it will help me. What he did wasn't love, it was torture. That's not BDSM, Enda. It was a sick, sick man getting off on hurting me. If you and I tried something ...well, that's kind of hot ..."

They were both distracted then by the building excitement in them both as they moved quicker, his cock driving deeper and deeper until Ama gave a cry of release, arching her back. The sight of her lovely body reacting to him made Enda come too, shooting thick streams of creamy cum into her belly.

"God, Ama ...let's promise never to stop doing this."

Ama was breathless, but she laughed. "I think I can safely guarantee that."

LATER, as they sat on the beach with Serafina, watching her play happily and chatter away to herself, Enda drew his fingers down Ama's spine. She shivered with pleasure.

"*Cara mia,* I was thinking. Maybe we should go away for a long weekend, somewhere we can experiment."

Ama squinted, as the sun got in her eyes when she turned to him. "Maybe we should. I've heard of places where people with certain kinks could go, but I'm not sure I'm ready to go that far."

"I was thinking more of a private island and a few toys that we both choose beforehand."

Ama's pulse began to race. "Now that I could get on board with." She looked at Serafina. "Although, leaving the munchkin for four whole days ..."

Enda laughed. "I have an idea who would be more than willing to have her for a long weekend."

"*Inca,*" they both said together and laughed.

. . .

THEY WERE RIGHT; Inca was overjoyed. Raffaelo pretended to be fed up, but secretly, Enda could tell he was delighted.

"Of course we'll have her. Hey, Sera, want to stay with your Auntie Inca for a few days?"

Sera bobbed her head and smiled. "Can I play with Fraggle?" Fraggle was the giant German Shepard Raffaelo had bought Inca to help with her protection when he was away. Raff often moaned that Inca had spoiled the dog so much, always cuddling him and giving him treats, that he was the worst guard dog ever. The dog also loved kids, which was handy when Raff and Inca's seven nieces and nephews came to stay.

"Definitely, Sera. I'm sure Fraggle will insist on it."

THE DAY CAME when Ama had to relinquish her daughter to her friend and fly to the private island where Enda had hired a villa for them. She hugged Serafina tightly, ignoring the amused glances of her husband and her friends. "Be good for Auntie Inca, won't you, nugget?"

Sera nodded merrily. "Have a nice vacation, Mama."

Ama's heart swelled with love. "Did Papa teach you to say that?"

Sera smiled. "And Auntie Inca, too." She gave her mother a wet kiss on the cheek. "Papa says I'm not to worry about you, that I will have a lovely time while you're gone. Is that right, Papa?"

Enda stroked his daughter's curls. "That's right, cara mia. Come give your Papa a hug."

AMA LOOKED out of the plane's window. Raff had lent them his private jet to fly out to the island in the Indian Ocean, and Ama, although she had come from a wealthy family and then married into one, still couldn't get used to the opulence of her surroundings.

"This is nothing," Enda said, enjoying her fascination with the jet. "Wait until you see the island."

"You've been there before?" Suddenly she felt jealous. Had he gone with another woman?

Enda, seeing the wariness in her eyes, smiled. "I went there with Raffaelo, Tommaso, and some of our friends for Raff's Bachelor party. When I say party, I'm talking eight middle-aged men listening to jazz, drinking whiskey, and playing cards for two days, albeit in luxury surroundings."

"Thug life."

Enda laughed. "You got it. We even stayed up past midnight one night."

Ama giggled. "You crazy kids. So ...no women?"

"No women. But I did get to thinking maybe it was somewhere I'd like to take someone I was in love with. Thankfully, for me at least, I've only ever been in love with one woman."

Ama pretended to be affronted. "Where is this bitch?"

Enda grinned, then pulled her onto his lap. "She's right here."

Ama smiled happily and leaned against him. "God, we're lucky."

"No arguments here. And guess what ...there's a bedroom back there." He nodded to the rear of the plane.

"There is?"

"Oh yes."

"And we're wasting time, sitting here chatting?"

"Now that you mention it ..."

Ama got up and held out her hand. "Take me to bed and fuck me senseless, husband."

Enda stood grinning. "You really are a very dirty girl ..."

"Well, doesn't that make you the lucky one?" And she led him towards the bedroom.

BACK IN ITALY, Raffaelo, who had been working in the city, drove home to find Inca and Serafina had built what turned out to be an intricate pillow fort in their living room. Fairy lights were strung inside, and Inca and Sera were lying on their backs, looking up at them. Raff poked his head inside and grinned at them. "Good evening, ladies."

They smiled back at him. Inca beckoned him. "Kick off your shoes and come join us."

Raff did as she asked, removing his jacket too, then crawled inside the building. "I must say, I'm very impressed with this fort." He suddenly felt a wet lick on his right ear. Fraggle was lying in a tunnel off the main 'living area' of the fort. "Hey, dog."

Fraggle gave a muffled 'woof,' which made Inca and Sera laugh. Raff grinned at them. "I think this kind of building deserves pizza, yes?"

Sera cheered, and Inca laughed at the girl's merry face. "Girl's got her priorities right in life. Come on, squidgy. Let's go help your uncle order."

THEY ATE the pizza in the fort, then sat playing games with Sera all evening. When the girl was falling asleep in Inca's arms, she carried her to bed in the guest room, tucked her in, and stroked her soft hair. Inca felt her heart hurt; if only she had been able to have kids of their own. She longed for a little girl like Sera, or her niece, Hermione, Tommaso's daughter.

The worst thing was that after being stabbed the first time, the doctors had told her she was highly unlikely to be able to carry her own child. Then, when she was attacked the second time ...she had unknowingly been pregnant. To save her life, though, they'd had to perform a hysterectomy, and their baby had died. Inca blinked back a few tears now. It wasn't fair. After everything they had been through together ...

"You okay, *Principessa*?"

Raff was standing in the doorway, watching them. Inca brushed her cheeks free of tears.

"Yes, baby. Just ..."

"I know."

They went back to their bedroom and stripped before sliding into the crisp sheets and wrapping themselves around each other. Raff brushed her lips with his. "What are you thinking about, *cara mia*?"

Inca smiled a little sadly. "Our little bean. How unfair it was that she was taken from us. I'm still so angry, Raff."

His arms tightened around her. "Maybe it's time to talk again about adoption."

Inca hesitated. "Aren't we too old now? Is that what they'll say?"

Raff shook his head. "I don't see why. Look, let's begin the process and we'll see what happens."

Inca smiled. "Okay ..."

Raff moved on top of her, then, smiling down at her. "You'll make an excellent mother, Inca, my darling."

"Let's not get our hopes up," she warned, but then sighed happily as Raff's cock slid into her. "For tonight, let's just concentrate on this ...us ...god, Raff, that feels so *good* ..."

THOUSANDS OF MILES AWAY, in the Indian Ocean, Ama was being shown around the luxurious villa that Enda had procured for them. At the center of the villa, was an enormous open-plan living room, dining room, and kitchen with one wall of sliding glass doors that led out onto a private beach. Ama went to the window and pushed it open, breathing in the warm ocean air. Enda slid his arms around her waist.

"What do you think?"

She grinned at him. "It'll do." They both laughed. "Seriously, this place is fantastic."

Enda showed her around the rest of the villa, including the master bedroom with a huge four-poster bed, swathed in white mosquito netting. Ama's heart began to beat faster ...god, this was perfect. Enda, carrying their suitcases, dropped them to the floor and ran his hand down her bare back before his fingers pulled at the halter-neck tie of her dress. The dress slithered down her body to the floor. Enda knelt and took her nipples into his mouth, teasing each tiny bud in turn. Ama sighed, caressing his head as his fingers stroked her belly and thighs before sliding between her legs to touch her, first through her panties. Then, as he drew them down her legs, his tongue found her clit.

Ama shivered with pleasure, giving a small moan, and Enda stood and swept her onto the bed. She unbuttoned his shirt, pushing it away from his broad, hard chest. Enda shrugged out of it, then out of his pants. He kissed her as she felt his cock, already hard and throbbing against her thigh. Enda grinned down at her. "Let's get this party started, *Piccolo* ..."

They kissed, tasted, sucked at each other until they were almost fevered with desire, and when Enda's cock thrust deep and hard into her, Ama cried out, saying his name over and over. He moved inside her, his hands pinning hers to the bed and his gaze locked onto her.

"What shall we try next, my love?" Enda was breathless, his eyes alive with desire as he moaned softly. Ama smiled up at him.

"Anything ...tie me up, Enda, and take me however you want."

"You want this?" He rammed his cock deeper into her, and she nodded. "God, yes, yes ..."

He fucked her into the most sublime orgasm, coming himself a second after and shooting creamy cum deep into her belly. He barely let her catch her breath before he was pulling out some silk ties from his suitcase, still on the floor at the side of the bed. "Come here, woman."

Ama giggled, only feeling a slight thrill of fear as Enda bound her wrists together and tied them to the bed. From the case, he pulled a long feather, which he ran over her skin. "You like this?"

Ama nodded. The tickle of the feather was almost unbearable; paired with Enda's fingers working her clit and the pull of the silk on her wrists, she could feel her body respond. Enda grinned, enjoying the control on her body. He grabbed a vibrator and switched it on, touching it gently to her clit. Ama shrieked as the vibration sent waves of pleasure through her already uber-sensitive clit. She could see Enda's cock, fully erect, bobbing under its own massive weight. "Let me suck you, baby ..."

Enda straddled her chest, and Ama took him into her mouth, sucking and teasing the sensitive tip, then running her tongue up and down the thick, long shaft. *"Mio Dio ..."* Enda whispered, "May I come in your sweet mouth, *Bella*?"

Ama nodded, her eyes shining, and Enda came, giving a groan and saying her name again and again. He withdrew and kissed her mouth, her throat, her breasts, and her belly. He nipped gently at the skin of her belly, then moved down to take her in his mouth. Ama writhed as he teased and suckled at her clit, then swept his tongue along her clit and plunged it deep into her cunt.

"Oh god ...god ...Enda!"

Enda grinned and leaned over to retrieve something else from the case—a huge glass dildo. Ama's eyes widened when she saw it. It was beautifully shaped, almost as big as Enda's cock, and had a ribbed section. Enda slid it into her as he continued to suck her clit, and soon Ama was moaning, her whole body vibrating with pleasure as she came hard.

Enda untied her wrists as she recovered, and Ama half-laughed, half-gasped as the circulation to her hands returned. Enda stroked the welts on her wrists. "And to think ...that was pretty tame bondage." He grinned at her. "Imagine what we *could* get up to."

Ama wriggled into his arms, snuggling her head against his chest. "We don't have to imagine ...we could just *do*."

Enda laughed. Outside, the evening was drawing in. "Well, just for now, I suggest we eat, b because I am starving, and then go for a moonlight walk."

"All the clichés."

"Hell, yes, *cara mia*. Every single one." He kissed her gently. *"Ti amo, Amalia."*

"Ti amo, Enda." Her stomach growled noisily and they both laughed. Enda got up and pulled her to her feet. "Come, wife. Let's eat."

. . .

INCA CARRIED Serafina into the tea house and was immediately greeted by her staff swooning over the child. Serafina was shy at first, but then basked in the attention. The customers fussed over her, too, but Inca, nervous, keep a watchful eye on the child. Even now, almost three years after she was attacked and stabbed downstairs in the tea house, she felt nervous when she came here. She hated that she was nervous—this teahouse had been her first in the city and had been where Raffaelo had proposed to her all those years ago.

"Now, who's this little beauty?"

Inca turned and smiled. Como, Raffaelo's friend, greeted her with a kiss on the cheek. "Ciao, *Bella.*"

"Ciao, Como. Can I get you some tea? Or juice?"

Como, a broad man who always wore impeccable suits, took his Panama hat off and sat down at her table. "Tea would be fine, thank you. How are you?"

Inca smiled at him. Como's occupation had never been clear to Inca, but she knew he operated both in the underworld and as a go-between for the polizia. When Raff had introduced them, soon after Inca was stabbed, Inca had thanked him for helping catch the men who tried to kill her. "I don't know what you do, Como, and I don't need to know. From this moment on, you are family."

He often visited her at the tea house; the other women teased her that Como was her sugar-daddy and they both found it hilarious, playing along. In reality, Inca felt like Como was a surrogate father-figure to her now. Her own adoptive father had been murdered and she'd never known her biological father. As Inca had settled into life in Italy, she found Como a comfort to be around.

He was shaking Sera's hand very seriously now as the little girl sized him up. Inca told him who Sera's parents were. He nodded. "Ah, yes ...I see the resemblance now." He smiled at Inca kindly. "Although, she could just as easily be yours."

Inca smiled sadly. "Raff and Enda could be twins and both Ama and I are of Indian ancestry." She paused, then lowered her voice. "Sometimes I feel like it's a cruel joke; showing me what my and Raff's child would have looked like, would have been. I love this little girl as if she were my own, but she's not." Her voice broke and she looked away, dashing tears from her eyes. "Sorry, Como."

He patted her hand. "Don't apologize, Inca. It's understandable."

Inca nodded, not trusting herself to speak for a long moment. Sera seemed to register her distress and climbed on her lap, studying her in the guileless, non-judgmental way only a child can. Inca smiled back through her tears.

"Don't cry, Inky," Sera said, matter-of-factly. "I'll give you a cuddle and that will make you feel better." She hugged Inca, who laughed softly.

"You were right. I do feel better, Sera. Thank you."

Como watched them. "Have you and Raff talked about adopting?"

"We have, but I'm scared of getting excited, only to be told we're too old or our pasts are too messy. We already know that Raff is past the age limit for adopting a baby." Inca sighed. "So I don't know, Como. It's something we'll have to make a decision on soon. Sometimes it's hard when we see Tommaso and Bo's troop of kids. So many of them at once." She laughed. "Those are usually the days when we're glad we *are* childless. But when we just have this little pickle with us ..." She hugged Sear tightly; the child was now occupied with playing with Como's cufflinks, which Inca guessed were probably worth more than this entire block of buildings.

Como studied Inca, an unreadable expression on his face. "It doesn't seem fair when you could give a child such a loving home."

Inca shrugged. "Those are the rules."

Como nodded slowly, then got up. His tea sat untouched on the table. Inca was surprised by his sudden movement. "I am sorry, Inca. I just remembered I have to be somewhere. Would you excuse me?"

LATER, at home, she wondered what had been going on in Como's mind, and she wished she hadn't blabbed her mouth so much. She felt guilty for dumping on him in a vulnerable moment. When Raffaelo came home, he could see she was preoccupied, and when Sera was tucked up in bed and asleep, he poured Inca and himself a glass of wine. They took it (and the ever-present baby monitor) out onto the terrace.

"Okay, *Bella,* let's hear it."

Inca told him about Como's visit. Raff listened, nodding, then sighed. "Knowing Como, he's trying to figure a way to get us the baby we want. I doubt if it'll work out. At least, not legally."

"And we can't use a surrogate because it'll be illegal here." Inca chewed her lip. "We'd have to move back to America."

Raff nodded. "And do you want to do that?"

"God, no." She smiled at him. "Look, maybe I'm just going through a phase. I love our life."

Raff reached over and stroked her hair. "Do you know how much I love you?"

She leaned into his touch. "I do. And I know you'd move heaven and Earth to give me a child. Some things weren't meant to be."

WHEN THEY WENT to bed that night, Inca fell asleep soon after love-making, but Raff couldn't sleep. He watched his beautiful wife, her beautiful body stretched out beside him. Raffaelo traced the scars on her belly from the stabbing—from *both* of her stabbings—and cursed the men who had put them there. He would give anything to see Inca's belly, without scars and round with his baby.

Anything ...

AMA FELT the steel of the handcuffs biting into her wrists and loved the pain of them. She lay on her stomach, bent over the back of the couch in the living room, while Enda stalked behind her, a riding crop in his hand and a cock ring around his ram-rod straight manhood. He brought the crop down on her buttocks and she yelped both with pain and pleasure.

"Louder!" Enda hissed at her, and she screamed his name. Enda thrust his cock deep into her cunt then and fucked her hard, pulling the handcuff so her back bent toward him as he took her.

Ama was delirious, lost completely in their game, and when she came, Enda pulled out and eased into her ass, fucking her slowly this time to prolong her pleasure. As he neared completion, he pulled out, flipping her onto her back and coming on her belly, then bringing the crop down, creating two red, angry strips across her abdomen.

They had been playing their games for two days now, completely uninhibited. Ama found she loved the sting of the whip, or the crop, so much that she would grow wet just thinking about it. Enda, kissing her, would slide his hands between her legs—she didn't bother with underwear here—and find her already so wet for him that he would take her wherever they were.

They spent the days—when they weren't fucking—exploring the island, swimming, and talking. They fucked against the trees in the forest, which was exhilarating until a giant spider dropped onto Ama's shoulder and she screamed bloody murder. Enda hadn't been able to breathe, he was laughing so hard, much to Ama's chagrin. She had immediately placed a sex-ban on him ...which had lasted for a whole ten minutes until they got back to the villa and Enda informed her she had far too many clothes on.

On the last day of their holiday, they lazed around in the pool, the sun beating down on their bare skin. Enda kissed Ama, and she smiled at him.

"*Piccolo*, have you enjoyed yourself?"

"So much. I'm just sorry we can't do this at home. But I think, with Sera in the house, I wouldn't feel comfortable or enjoy it so much."

Enda kissed her shoulder. "I agree. But, *Bella*, we must make a pact. One a year, maybe twice, we come here and do this."

Ama grinned and wrapped her arms around his neck. "I think I can agree to that. Thank you, Enda ...thank you for being the one person I can trust above all else, the one person who I know loves me beyond doubt."

Enda grinned. "I think there's two of us now, but I'll take the compliment." His face grew serious. "Has it helped? I mean, has it erased some of the trauma from what Jackson did to you?"

Ama nodded. "Believe me, this was a different world. This was about connection and love and adventure; that was torture. Opposite end of the spectrum."

Enda pressed his mouth to hers. "I'm glad, Amalia. So glad."

Ama smiled at him, tears in her eyes. "You make me so happy."

And she pulled him into the deepest part of the pool.

INCA'S EYES widened when she saw Raff coming into the tea house in the middle of the day. "Well, this is a pleasant surprise ...but what are you doing here?"

Raff kissed her hello. "No idea. Como called me and asked me to come here to meet him."

Inca frowned. "Weird." But when Como walked in five minutes later, accompanied by a very young, very pregnant young woman, Inca's heart sank. She knew exactly what this was about.

Como saw her face and held up his hands. "Before you say anything, let me explain. Anitha is desperate. She wants to give her child to a good, kind couple. The baby's father is

"STOP." Raff looked astonished. "What's this about?"

Inca sighed, rubbing her forehead. "It's about us not being able to adopt a baby. Como, you are the sweetest man, but this is not the solution. Anitha, you look pale. Come sit down."

She got the young woman to sit and brought her some tea, shaking her head at Como as she walked past. "What are you thinking?"

Como looked disappointed. "Look, Anitha's mother is my friend. For months now, they have been trying to decide what to do. They're illegal immigrants, so giving up the child to the authorities would raise questions. I thought ...it would solve two people's problems."

Inca sat down next to Anitha. She was obviously of Indian

descent, too, and smiled shyly at Inca. Inca patted her hand. "Anitha ...do you really want to give up your baby?"

Anitha shot a worried glance at Como, but shook her head. "But we cannot afford to keep it," she said in a heavily accented voice. "I cannot work and my boyfriend, he doesn't earn enough for rent, let alone a baby too. We have to be practical."

Inca's heart broke for the girl. She glanced at Raff and an unspoken connection passed between them. Inca sighed. "Look, Anitha, Como ...we can't be party to an illegal adoption. That's not something we would ever consider. But we need to talk, Raff and I. Como, can you bring Anitha back tomorrow and we'll tell you what we've decided?"

AT HOME, Raffaelo and Inca talked until the early hours, then fell asleep in each other's arms, satisfied they were making the right decision for them.

"IF I WEREN'T SO desperate to see Sera, I'd be loathed to get on this plane," Ama said as they found their seats ready for the flight back to Italy. Enda laughed.

"I agree. But don't forget ...we'll be back sooner than later."

Ama wiggled her eyebrows at him suggestively. "With new toys, maybe."

"Dirty girl."

Ama grinned and put her hand on his leg. "I am what you made me."

Enda tried to argue, but instead leaned over and kissed her. "To next year, *cara mia*."

Ama smiled back, her eyes soft with love. "To next year. Or sooner," she added hopefully and then laughed as the plane took off and carried them home.

. . .

INCA TOOK ANITHA'S HANDS. "Sweetheart, we're not going to take your baby. It wouldn't be right for any of us. What we are going to do is help you and your boyfriend. Raff is going to hire your boyfriend to work in one of his hotels, and when you're ready, there's a job waiting for you too." She looked at Raff, who nodded, smiling. "And when you want to go back to work, you can count on me helping out with caring for the baby. We'll get you back on track, okay? This isn't charity; we expect your boyfriend to work his ass off. But everyone needs a break sometimes, and we are in a position to be able to help with that."

She took a deep breath in as Anitha stammered and thanked her. Inca met Raff's gaze and nodded. They knew they had made the right decision. So, kids weren't for them. But they would make sure Anitha's child, even though she was a stranger to them, had a good start in life. A chance, Raff had said, and Inca had agreed.

Como was looking at Inca with respect in his eyes. She got up and hugged him. "I know you meant well, Como, and for that, I thank you."

She let out a deep breath. "And now, I'm afraid, we have to deliver this little pest." She mussed Sera's hair fondly. "She goes back to her mom and dad. Ama and Enda should be home any minute."

AMA FLEW OUT of the car and gathered her daughter up in her arms, swinging her around. "Oh, nugget, I missed you."

"Not that much," Enda joked in a stage-whisper. Sera stuck her tongue out at her dad, knowing he was teasing her. He took Sera from his wife's arms and hugged her. Ama embraced Inca.

Inca smiled at them both. "Well, don't you look ...*radiant*." She grinned, obviously guessing exactly what they had done on their vacation. Ama smiled and winked at her.

"You know it."

Sera moaned to be held by her mother again, so Enda handed her over. "Have you been good for Auntie Inca?"

Sera nodded. "Auntie Inca was going to have a baby, then the lady said she wanted to keep it, so Auntie Inca said she would give the girl a job and her boyfriend needed to give his ass away, or it would fall off."

Inca gaped at Sera as Enda and Raff burst into laughter. Ama looked both amused and confused. She grinned at Inca's red face and nodded towards her daughter. "Ears on sticks, brains like sponges," she told her friend and tucked her hand under Inca's arm.

"How about we go inside and talk about it?"

And the two families—who were really one family—went inside to talk, and laugh, and love.

THE END.

ABOUT THE AUTHOR

Mrs. Love writes about smart, sexy women and the hot alpha billionaires who love them. She has found her own happily ever after with her dream husband and adorable 6 and 2 year old kids. Currently, Michelle is hard at work on the next book in the series, and trying to stay off the Internet.

"Thank you for supporting an indie author. Anything you can do, whether it be writing a review, or even simply telling a fellow reader that you enjoyed this. Thanks

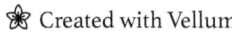 Created with Vellum

CPSIA information can be obtained
at www.ICGtesting.com
Printed in the USA
BVHW041405100221
599801BV00005B/109